W9-CLG-615

TIME AND PLACE

BOOKS
BY BRYAN WOOLLEY

We Be Here When the Morning Comes
Some Sweet Day

Time AND Place

BRYAN WOOLLEY

THOMAS CONGDON BOOKS | E. P. DUTTON | NEW YORK

Library of Congress Cataloging in Publication Data

Woolley, Bryan.
Time and place.

"Thomas Congdon books."
I. Title.
PZ4.W918Ti [PS3573.067]   813'.5'4   76–58873
ISBN: 0–525–21991–9
Published simultaneously in Canada by Clarke, Irwin & Company
Limited, Toronto and Vancouver

10 9 8 7 6 5 4 3 2 1
First Edition

FOR MY BROTHERS AND SISTERS

And I will give unto thee
and to thy seed after thee,
the land wherein thou art a stranger . . .

AUGUST, 1952

One

On the sheep ranches, the brittle grass was grazed to its roots. The sheep men had ruined their land, the cow men said. Not even rain would help.

But the cow land wasn't much better. A few cow men who had the money had bought hay and hauled it to their pastures. They watched, almost in tears, as their gaunt Herefords trudged to their pickups while wetbacks cut the wires on the bales and pushed the hay into the dust. Some hauled water for a while. Some just let their beasts starve and fill the bellies of buzzards. Some joked of asking for government loans to buy ammunition to shoot their herds.

The cow men and the sheep men and their foremen and their hands and even the people in town still worried over Eisenhower's decision to run as a Republican. The Democrats had nominated a man they had never heard of and didn't understand. Until now, voting Republican had seemed as impossible as moving to Russia or joining the Communist Party. But Governor Shivers was going to vote for Ike, and they knew they would, too. He had promised to go to Korea. Stevenson was no FDR, after all. No Harry Truman, even. They would vote for Ike, and hope they were betraying nothing.

It was the worst polio year yet, the newspapers said. Not in Fort Appleby, of course. But Fort Appleby people read the stories in the *Fort Worth Star-Telegram* and the *El Paso Times*. They shook their heads over their coffee at the drugstore. More and more people were driving from San Antonio and Houston and Dallas and Odessa and El Paso, buying small tracts at the foot of Leaping Panther Mountain and building summer houses on them, fleeing the iron lungs and the death. Elmer Martin, who ran the drugstore, said the Houston people and the ants were taking over the town.

None of this bothered Eduardo Rodriguez. Despite drought and war and politics and disease, he loved the last days of August more than any other time of year. The schoolhouse was like a bride on the eve of her wedding, rid of the loneliness of the long summer, bright with expectation, but still a virgin. Eduardo was the bride's mother. He was proud that his work was about to be seen and appreciated by the town, but he knew that after Labor Day the building would no longer belong to him, its virginal glow would be gone, and he would be stuck with its problems. In the last days of August, though, there were no problems, and the beauty was all his.

He had sanded, varnished, and waxed the yellow oak floors of the classrooms. He had scrubbed the slate blackboards to their pristine gray. The windows gleamed. The new coat of white on the walls of the corridors and classrooms glowed coolly around their light green woodwork. Since 1925, when the building was new and he was young, Eduardo had never changed the color of the woodwork. He had been to other schools for basketball tournaments and football games, and had seen the ugly chocolate brown of their door facings and windowsills. It concealed the dirt and vandalism of the children, their janitors said. Eduardo sneered at them. Only in 1939, when that AK was carved on the wall of the boys' rest room's second stall, had a single Fort Appleby student dared take a knife to Eduardo's woodwork. Eduardo had hated Albert Kirk for that, and of all the Fort Appleby children who had fallen in the big war, Eduardo had mourned Albert least. But now Eduardo suspected that it was God who moved Albert to cut so deep. He had no family, no good works, no grave. Everyone is entitled to leave some mark on the world.

Eduardo stood at the end of the corridor of the high-school wing and gazed down the line of steel lockers to the front door. Every locker door and latch worked as well in 1952 as it had in 1925. The red stone floor, waxed and polished to a dangerous sheen, reflected the shafts of sunlight that shot through the open classroom doors. This gaze of pride down the cleanliness and beauty of his domain had become an annual ritual for Eduardo in recent years, a kind of pre-school meditation on the lives of all the children who had entered his building as little more than babies and left it twelve years later as adults. There was no teacher left who could remember as many of them as he. He could recall the locker numbers of some of them.

Eduardo dragged his steel Westclox from the bib pocket of his overalls and held it at the length of its shoestring. It was time for lunch. He propped his heavy pushbroom against the lockers and shuffled down the long corridor that connected the high school to the Anglo elementary-school wing. He peered in the door of the library. Mrs. Overby was sitting on the floor, dressed in a man's white shirt and red pedalpushers, a costume that Eduardo considered ridiculous on a grandmother.

"Not through?" he asked quietly.

She looked up from her pile of battered volumes and glue pots and mending tape. Her glasses perched too low on her nose. A strand of gray hair stuck to her sweating forehead.

"Afraid not," she replied. "Some of these books are as old as the school, and show it."

Eduardo, suspecting that his building had been insulted somehow, stiffened. "I need to clean up in here," he said.

5

Mrs. Overby raised her eyebrows and sniffed. "Don't worry, Eduardo. School doesn't open until Tuesday."

Eduardo passed on, angry at himself for stopping and endangering his August mood. Next door in the principal's office, Jay Eisenbarger was talking on the telephone. He waved at Eduardo as he passed. A good man, Eduardo considered him, although he sometimes put his feet on his desk.

Eduardo paused at the trophy cases. He enjoyed the soft glow of the gold and silver metal in the corridor's shadows. He had been in schools that kept the prizes of their athletic and academic triumphs on open shelves in the principal's office or the gymnasium, gathering dust and corroding. But Fort Appleby's every award, some of them older than the building itself, rested clean and proud behind glass in the cases that Eduardo had built. He worried sometimes about the trophies that would be won after his cases were full and he was gone. "There is an obligation . . ." he would think at those times. But he had never completed the thought.

He stepped through the back door of the elementary wing, into the sunlight. He squinted, wishing he had remembered his hat, glad that he had nothing more to do outdoors before school started, except keep the sprinklers running on the football field.

The field, except for the schoolhouse itself, was Eduardo's proudest achievement. It was the only grassy field in Fort Appleby's district, and he gloated silently on those Saturday mornings when he found players in the drugstore, moaning to each other about the bruises and cuts they had suffered the previous afternoon on the stony, dusty field at Geneva or Fort Henderson or Castalon. Fort Appleby people beamed at the envy of out-of-towners who came to watch their sons fall on Eduardo's grass. It was worth all the water it required. Someday, Eduardo hoped, there would also be some bleachers.

He trudged across the gravel playground, his head bowed to protect his eyes from the glare. He crossed the dusty road and entered his backyard. The heavy spring on his wooden gate pulled it shut with a solid *swak*. He raised his head now, in the shade of the elms his father had planted. He inhaled deeply, drawing into his nostrils the wet, sweet odor of the two large fig trees by the windmill. That odor and the shadows of the elm leaves and branches dancing across the cobbled patio and the lawn meant home to him in summer, as the oak logs blazing in his fireplace did in winter. He wasn't yet born when his father planted the elms, but he had helped when the patio was laid. He remembered how heavy the stones had been in his arms.

"Eduardo?"

"Yes?"

"It's ready."

He climbed the stone steps and opened the screen door. Juanito, clad only in white underpants, rushed him and grabbed his knees. Eduardo laughed and grabbed the boy under the arms and lifted him, flipped him, and held him upside down by the ankles.

The child giggled as if he had been tickled. "Let's eat, Grandpa!" he yelled.

"Yes," Dolores said. "The tortillas are getting cold."

A steaming pot of *frijoles*, a plate heaped with sliced tomatoes, green onions, and green peppers, a towel-covered pan of tortillas, and tall, sweating glasses of iced tea were ready on the blue-oilcloth-covered table at the end of the porch, where the ivy covered the screen. Eduardo flipped Juanito again and swung him onto the cane-bottomed chair with the two thick pillows on it, between his grandparents' places.

"It's a hot day," Eduardo said, seating himself and pulling the bean pot toward him.

"Yes," Dolores replied. "I don't remember a hotter summer."

"There have been others."

"Yes. But I don't remember them. It's the drought, too, I think."

"Umm. Where's Gilberto working today?"

"They started a new job. For one of the summer people. They're adding a room."

"So late in the year?"

Dolores shrugged. "I guess they want to have it ready for next year."

"When's Ernestina coming for the boy?"

"She went to Sharon. There's a sale at Bronski's. Gilberto will get him after he gets off."

Eduardo watched his grandson gnaw a tortilla. Butter dripped from one corner of the boy's small mouth.

"I don't remember a hotter summer," Dolores said, wiping her brown forehead with her napkin. "Maybe I'm just getting old."

Eduardo smiled. "Maybe. Your hair's getting gray."

Dolores's round face crinkled into a coquettish smile. "But not as gray as yours, old man. I'll have a chance at plenty of men after you're gone."

"Because of your cooking only."

Dolores laughed, her large bosom quivering under her flowered apron. "Old fool!" she said. "You know nothing. Grandpa doesn't know anything, does he, Juanito?"

"He knows *everything!*" the child yelled, shaking his black curls.

"Smart kid," Eduardo said. "For that, you get ice cream after work."

"*Now!*"

"No, after work. If you don't bother my nap."

"How's it going?" Dolores asked.

"It's almost ready, except for the library. Old Lady Overby won't leave."

"What's she doing?"

"Messing up the floor with glue and tape and little pieces of paper."

Dolores hissed sharply and shook her head. "Some people," she said.

Eduardo ate heartily and poured down three glasses of the sweet, lemony iced tea. Then he wiped his mouth and fingers with the white cloth napkin and pushed himself away from the table. His chair legs scraped harshly across the rough floorboards. "I'm going to rest now," he said. He pointed a calloused finger at his grandson's nose. "You, too, boy."

Juanito's face puckered. "I want the ice cream now," he whimpered. "My throat hurts."

"Then you need medicine. Not ice cream."

"No! Ice cream!"

"A nap first. It'll make you feel better."

"No!"

"No nap, no ice cream," Eduardo said. He walked quickly through the kitchen, still hot and heavy with the odors of beans and onions, into the long, dark hallway, leaving Dolores to deal with Juanito's whining. He turned into the living room, crossed to the green daybed by the corner windows, and lay down. He could hear Dolores cooing to Juanito. He hoped the child's throat wasn't really sore. If he got a cold now, it would last all winter. Maybe it was just the dryness, and the dust.

The windowshades had been down all day, and the room was almost as dark as a cave, and as cool. Two-foot-thick adobe walls. Fourteen-foot ceiling. There was no reason for people to be uncomfortable in Fort Appleby in the summer, Eduardo knew, if they built their houses right. His father had known how, and he had the money in those days. Eduardo's was one of the largest homes in Fort Appleby. The largest Mexican home to this day.

The back screen door slammed, and the voices of Dolores and Juanito faded into the afternoon. Eduardo knew that Dolores had given in to Juanito's whining. They were walking to the drugstore. Eduardo considered rising and bringing them back, insisting that his authority be respected, demanding that the child take his nap. But he decided not to, and sighed. His eyes wandered to the wall above the mantelpiece. He worried about his father's buffalo robe, hanging there with his Henry rifle and his spurs. Little tufts of hair had fallen out. That shouldn't be allowed to happen to the possessions of a man who had driven stagecoaches, had fought Indians, had been friends with colonels. Perhaps he should build a glass case . . .

When Eduardo awoke and stepped into the road again, his head lowered against the sun, he didn't hear the engine. The horn's blast made his heart leap. He lost his balance and almost fell into the path of the car. It swerved slightly, and the driver smiled and waved as he flashed by. Eduardo stared after him, squinting into the cloud of dust.

Two

Jasper Birdsong slouched behind the wheel of the black 1940 Ford. The Ford's old engine rumbled lustily through the fiberglass muffler, in perfect tune. He revved it, enjoying the noise of each cylinder's explosion tumbling over the noise of the others. He peered again at the ivy-colored front porch of the Adams house, then honked. Kevin Adams trotted down the sidewalk and slid his long, lanky form into the front seat. A grin lit his small blue eyes and etched a single deep line at each corner of his wide mouth. "Keep your shirt on, buddy," he said.

Jasper gunned the car back into the street. Kevin turned and looked at the blue plaid seatcovers. They reeked of plastic and were still creased where they had been folded into their box. "Nice," he said.

"Yeah, and I don't want you getting any spots on that back seat, either."

"Spots?"

"Mustard. Beer. Pussy-juice. Nothing."

Kevin pulled out a cigarette and lit it. Jasper reached for one, too, and Kevin held the match for him. The blue curlicues of smoke reminded him of the training rules that he and Jasper would break again this year. "Well, this time next week we'll be suiting up again," he said.

"Yeah. Too bad we have to go to school to play football."

"Remember what Mr. Jay says, buddy. 'Man works, in order to have the right to play.' "

"Shit! Eisenbarger never played in his life. I bet he's at home right now, thinking up term theme topics."

Jasper lounged gracefully behind the steering wheel, his left elbow resting on the sill of the open window, his right

11

hand grasping the red plastic steering knob. He jerked the knob to the right, nosing the Ford into the narrow lane to the Birdsongs' town house, a Victorian sandstone that stood four hundred yards off the highway. The brown, grassy pasture between the house and the highway was fenced with barbed wire, and in the middle of the pasture, fifty yards from the lane, stood a windmill, its wheel turning slowly now in the hot breeze. Beside the windmill stood a rusty steel tank, seven feet tall. Jasper pulled over and stopped.

"Is it full?" Kevin asked.

"Don't know. I haven't seen it since the last time you were with me."

The boys crawled out of the car and climbed the fence. The long, dry grass swished against their Levis as they walked toward the windmill, sidestepping prickly pear and Spanish dagger, detouring around the U-shaped stand of pea-green mesquite that hid the tank from the highway and part of the lane.

"Man, listen to that!" Kevin said. The rhythmic splash of water drawn from the cool innards of the earth sent a shiver up his sweaty back.

Jasper broke into a run, tearing at the snaps on his cowboy shirt. He arrived at the tank half-naked, flung his shirt onto the thorns of a mesquite, and scrambled up the crude, scrap-lumber ladder that he and Kevin had nailed together and propped against the tank three summers ago. He balanced himself on one foot at the top of the ladder, yanking at a boot. Kevin undressed slowly, grinning at Jasper's frenzy. Jasper flung his white shorts at Kevin and stepped from the ladder to the weathered two-by-twelve that they had laid a long time ago across an arc of the circular tank's thin rim. "Hey, it's almost full! Beautiful!" he cried. He raised his brown arms like an Indian praying and let himself fall face down into the cool green water. His splash shot clear drops over the edge, wetting Kevin's short, sandy hair. Kevin, sniffing the water-smell, hurried now. When he reached the top of the ladder, Jasper was already floating on his back near the center of the disk of opaque green, undulating gently among the waves his fall had made. From behind strands of long, stringy black hair he grinned.

"Cover your ass," Kevin said, clamping his nostrils shut with thumb and forefinger. He jumped as high and far as he could and lifted his knees toward his chin. His pale body cannonballed into the water only inches from Jasper, who went under, too. They came up together, sputtering and laughing, rubbing their eyes. "I *told* you to cover your ass," Kevin said. Four quick strokes propelled him to the far side of the tank. He grabbed one of the two black truck inner-tubes floating there, pulled it down, and lay back into it. Jasper jumped onto the other tube. They reclined like emperors, squinting into the translucent dome of robin's-egg sky.

Kevin closed his eyes. "Jesus, this is great," he said.

"Umm."

"Better than punching cows, huh?"

"Umm."

"Hey, you going to sleep?"

Jasper didn't answer. Kevin knew he was faking, but he, too, was falling under the spell of the tube's gentle rocking, the sun's warmth on his chest and legs, and the liquid cool on his back, crotch, and feet. "Hey, Jasper," he said in a low, lazy voice that he knew would be answered.

"Hm?"

"Have you decided yet where you're going to school next year?"

"Princeton."

"Princeton!"

13

"Yeah. My old man still wants me to go to A&M. But I'd rather be an Ivy Leaguer."

Kevin smiled. "I bet you wind up at A&M."

"I'd hate it. All those cows and Army uniforms . . ."

"You'll love it."

"Shit. I want to get out of Texas. I want to go where something's happening."

"Aggie Land isn't Fort Appleby High, you know."

"It isn't Princeton, either." He sighed. "Who the fuck knows what I'm going to do? What are *you* going to do?"

"Go to school, I hope."

"Where?"

"Wherever I can get a job. Not Princeton. Texas Western, maybe."

"Shit. I'll miss you up there." Jasper grinned lazily, his eyes still closed. "We could have some good old times up there, ripping and romping around New York. We would turn that town on its goddamn *ear!*"

Kevin frowned. "It's easier to get laid in El Paso. In Juarez, anyway. It would get you out of Texas, too. They've got girls there who'll take you around the world for five bucks."

Jasper's giggle reverberated against the tank walls. "Fuck Princeton!" He peered at Kevin. "What if you can't find a job?"

"Then it's the Army, I guess."

"And Korea."

"Yeah, I guess."

"Shit."

"Why don't you and I join up? *That* would get you out of Texas!"

"Shit, no! If the Army wants old Jasper, they're going to have to drag his ass out of these hills."

"A true patriot. Patrick Henry would be proud of you."

"Old Pat didn't have to fight Chinese. Next time we have a war with England, I'll be ready."

"Let's stop talking about that. Right now it's just school . . ."

"And football . . ."

"And basketball . . ."

"And track . . ."

"And beer . . ."

"And pussy . . ."

"God, I hope so!"

"Shh!"

"What?"

A whistle, sweet and wistful, drifted to them on the wind. "Oh, shit!" Jasper whispered. "Somebody's coming!"

"So what?"

"We're buck naked! What if it's a woman?"

"Women don't whistle."

They lay in their tubes, listening intently. The tune sounded Mexican. The whistler was moving toward them. They turned their eyes toward the ladder, sure now that a face would appear there. The whistling ceased at the foot of the ladder. Suddenly Kevin was aware of the rush of the breeze through the windmill's wheel, the splash of the dollops of water it was pulling into the tank, the ruffling of the feathers on the mockingbird that perched on the rim of the tank, cocked its head at the floating bodies for a moment, then fluttered away. The whistler was on the ladder now. The crown of his dirty straw hat appeared, then the brim, then the smiling freckled face of Emiliano Hawthorne.

"Hola," he said. "I saw your car."

"Hi, Emmy," Jasper replied. "You scared the shit out of us."

"Jasper thought you were a woman," Kevin said.

Emiliano smiled. "I'm not." He stepped onto the two-by-twelve and lay down on his side, leaning on his elbow. He tilted his hat back, uncovering dark red curls plastered with sweat to his forehead. Kevin hadn't seen him in nearly a year, since he turned sixteen and dropped out of school. He was heavier, and stronger-looking. His size, plus his sweaty, work-stained clothing and scuffed combat boots, made him appear older than Kevin felt. Kevin wondered if he had changed as much during the past year as Emiliano, and if anyone had noticed it.

"I didn't know you were coming to town," Jasper said.

"Your mama sent me for groceries."

"Shit, that's what I'm supposed to do!"

"Your mama said you would forget. There's also a saddle that your father wants from the house."

"Oh. They didn't tell me about that."

"They probably forget. That's why they sent me, I guess." His Mexican accent was thicker than Kevin remembered it.

"Hey, you coming back to school this year, Emmy?" Kevin asked.

"No."

"Why not?"

"I'd go to school. I'd graduate. I'd go to work for Jasper's father." He shrugged. "I already work for Jasper's father now."

"Jump in and swim awhile," Jasper said. "You look hot."

Emiliano gazed at him a moment, then shrugged. He stood up and peeled off his sweaty clothes and dropped them over the edge of the tank. He gazed down at the floating boys, his pale skin glistening in the sun. Then he jumped, his impact rocking the tubes like toy boats. He came up grinning and dog-paddled to Jasper and hung on to his tube.

"Great, huh?" Jasper said.

16

"Yes. But don't tell your father."

"Shit, no."

Emiliano tilted the tube and tossed Jasper into the water. He climbed aboard before Jasper could recover. Kevin paddled to Emiliano and grabbed him and wrestled him off of the tube. But he lost his own balance and fell into the water. The boys played king-of-the-mountain with the tubes, the tubeless one trying to unseat his opponents. They dived and wrestled, harassing one another, cursing, shouting, laughing. Then Emiliano swam to the two-by-twelve and abruptly pulled himself out of the water. He lay down in the sun.

"What's the matter, Emmy?" Jasper called. "You chickening out?"

"I've got to go. I've got work to do."

"Are you going to get the groceries?"

"Yeah."

"Then tell Mom I'll be late. Kevin and I are going to Sharon to drink some beer. Don't tell her that, though. Tell her we went to a picture show."

"Okay."

The sun dried Emiliano quickly, and he climbed down the ladder and dressed. Jasper and Kevin swam to the rim and waved at him as he walked away.

"Not a bad old Meskin," Jasper said.

"I like him."

"You want some beer?"

"Sure."

"Let's go to Sharon."

"I don't have any money."

"I'll loan you some."

"Okay. But I'll have to call my mother."

In fifteen minutes the black Ford was roaring down the narrow, curving highway to Sharon, twenty-five miles down the canyons from Fort Appleby. The windows were open, and the wind was strong in the boys' faces, but their backs were sweating against the plastic seatcovers.

"Jesus, it must be close to a hundred today," Jasper said.

"Yeah, even the wind is hot. I don't remember another summer like this."

Jasper didn't reply. He was listening to the pop of the exhaust as the Ford coasted down the long hairpin turn and then hit the straightaway to the town shimmering in the distance. Jasper floorboarded the accelerator, and the old car shook as if about to fly apart. Its doors rattled in their latches. Kevin turned on the radio, but could find nothing but static and turned it off again. "Your radio's not worth a shit," he said.

"I'm going to fix it one of these days. God, that beer's going to taste good!"

At the edge of town, he wheeled into one of the shedlike parking spaces at Cisco's Drive-In and squealed to a stop. "You get the beer," he said.

"Shit, you always make me do that!"

"You look older than me." He handed Kevin a five-dollar bill as a short, fat Mexican man slammed the screen door and waddled to the car. He came to Kevin's side.

"A case of Lone Star," Kevin said, trying to sound nonchalant.

The Mexican glanced toward a pickup parked two spaces from the car. Three cowboys were sitting in it, their hats tilted back, drinking. One was peering at the Ford. "Drive to the back door," the Mexican said.

Jasper started the engine and drove slowly around the corner to the kitchen entrance. The garbage can beside the door was open and stinking. Jasper kept the engine running, tapping the accelerator lightly with his toe, until the Mexican came out carrying an open-topped cardboard box filled with cans of beer. He walked around the car to Kevin's side.

"Is it cold?" Kevin asked.

"Sure. Always."

"Did you put a churchkey in?"

"Yes."

"How much?"

"Six dollars."

"Jesus Christ!"

The Mexican shrugged. "Six dollars."

Jasper dug into his pocket for another dollar and handed it to Kevin. The Mexican passed the beer through the window, and Kevin handed him the money. The Mexican nodded. "I hope your fathers enjoy the beer," he said. He grinned, then walked around the rear of the car and into the drive-in.

"That robber!" Jasper said.

"He knows we're underage. I guess he figures he's taking a risk."

"Shitass!"

"Well, we got it, anyway. What now?"

"You want to find some girls?"

"Shit, no. I hate these goddamn Sharon girls. They're all so stuck up, like they were from Dallas or something."

"Okay, let's go out to the roadside park, and sit around and drink beer, and when it gets dark we'll go to a picture show. How about that?"

"Lead on, buddy."

Jasper drove slowly down the main street of the town, past the Hotel Oldham, past Snapper's Chevron Service and Thompson Auto Parts and Sharon Do-Nut Shoppe and Helen's Flowers & Gifts and the SharonView Drive-In Theater to the roadside park on the highway to Castalon. A semi was pulled up beside the concrete picnic table. Its driver's feet protruded from the window. "If he wakes up, we'll give him a beer," Jasper said. He passed the semi and parked alongside a row of yuccas that the Highway Department had planted along the stone curb. "Give me one."

Kevin pressed the churchkey into the can. The beer spewed like a geyser. Kevin held it out the window, away from the new seatcovers. "Jesus," he said. When the geyser died, he handed the can to Jasper and opened another, more slowly this time. He sucked at the V-shaped hole and shivered at the cold, bitter taste. "God," he said, "beer's great."

"Yeah, I feel sorry for teetotalers. How do they celebrate anything?"

"My mother celebrates with Cokes."

"Those can't get you happy. How can you celebrate anything without getting drunk?"

"You can't. Not like we can. What are we celebrating?"

"Let's see." Jasper combed his long black hair with his fingers. "The drought? No. The beginning of school? Hell, no. The end of school? How about that? We'll celebrate our graduation. We'll drink to the future."

Kevin grinned. He raised his can. "Here's to the future! To Jasper Birdsong, future hot shit on the Circle-B, future daddy of two beautiful *gringo* kids and fifteen Meskins!"

"Shit, Kevin, you got it *wrong!* I'm going to be a movie star!"

"Oh. Then here's to the John Wayne of the future!"

"Shit, no! Rock Hudson! Cary Grant! I'm not going to ride any fucking horses. I'm going to fuck Doris Day and Ingrid Bergman and have whole fan clubs full of tight little cunts. That's *my* future. What's yours?"

"Maybe *I'll* be hot shit on the Circle-B, then. I'll change the brand to Circle-A."

"No shit? Is that what you want?"

"No, I want to be a writer. Like Hemingway. I want to go to Spain and Africa and do all that writer shit. They can make movies of my novels, and you can star in them. How about that?"

"We got it, buddy! That's the future I'll drink to!"

They sat and drank and smoked, watching the sun disappear behind the mountains in the blue distance, gazing at the truckdriver's feet protruding from the window of his cab, never moving. They stopped talking. They just opened the beers and drank them, lit the cigarettes and smoked them, letting the alcohol flow to their fingertips and make them tingle. Jasper massaged his temples with his fingers. He blinked hard several times. Then, out of a twilight distance, he said, "I think that fucker's dead."

"Naw, he's just asleep. Let's go get something to eat and see what the picture shows are."

Jasper turned toward Kevin. His eyes were glazed, his jaw slack. "I hate to do this, friend," he said thickly, "but I think I better go home. I feel like shit."

"What's the matter?"

"I got a headache that won't quit. I think you better drive."

"You're drunk."

"I never felt like this before. I feel like shit. I mean it."

Kevin got out and walked around to the driver's side. "Move over, Jasper. I'll take care of you."

The Ford was stiff and unfamiliar under his hands, and he drove slowly. It was full dark when he reached Fort Appleby. The street was deserted. He drove through the town, up Victorio Canyon, and over the cattleguard. Jasper didn't speak, even while the Ford jolted over the rough dirt road to the headquarters house. Kevin was glad the house was dark. He wouldn't have to explain Jasper's condition to Mrs. Birdsong. He cut the engine and the lights and helped

21

Jasper up the steps and into his bedroom. He threw back the sheet and helped him into the bed. "Your folks aren't here," he said. "Can I do anything else?"

"No. Thanks, buddy," Jasper whispered.

"Your car will be at my house."

"Okay."

"Goodnight. Take care of yourself."

Jasper didn't answer. Kevin felt his way back through the dark house. He started the car and sped down the dirt road. He didn't want to encounter Jasper's parents, at least until he was on the highway again and could ignore them. He gunned the Ford down the canyon and was passing Little Juarez when his headlights caught the back of a girl, walking along the highway. He started to speed on, then recognized her and stopped. She peered at the car. "Jasper?"

"No, Kevin. Jasper got a little drunk."

The girl walked to the car and looked in. "Hi."

"Hi, Rosa. What you doing out here?"

"Just walking. The house was so hot."

"Climb in. We'll take a ride."

"Oh, I don't know, Kevin."

"Climb in. I'm not going to hurt you."

She sighed, and walked around the car and got in. Kevin sniffed her perfume. "You want a beer? It's probably pretty warm by now."

"No. I hate warm beer."

He slammed the Ford into gear, U-turned and headed back up Victorio Canyon.

"Why do you have Jasper's car?" she asked.

"He was too drunk to drive. I took him home."

He suddenly pulled off the highway onto a rough dirt road. He braked the Ford down the steep embankment toward Victorio Creek and stopped in a small clearing amid

22

a thicket of creek willows. The tops of beer cans that other parkers had left reflected the headlights like small moons. Then he pushed the switch and cut the engine.

"What are you doing?" Rosa asked.

"Parking," he replied. "I've got a pretty girl, and I'm parking."

"I don't think it's a good idea."

"Why not?" He put his arm around her shoulders, but she hunched forward and hugged her knees, avoiding his embrace.

"Jesus Christ, Rosa!"

"You're drunk. I don't park with just anybody."

"I'm not drunk. And I'm not just anybody."

"But I've never parked with you. And I don't think I should."

"Why not?"

"You know why not. Please."

She turned her face toward him, but he couldn't see her eyes in the darkness. "Jesus Christ, Rosa," he said. But he removed his hand from her shoulder and let it drop to the seat between them. "I like you."

She placed her hand on his. "I know," she said softly. "I'm glad. But not tonight. You're drunk."

"I'm not."

"I think you are. If I ever park with you, I want to be sure that you're not."

They sat in silence, he staring through the windshield at the dark willows, she holding his hand, gazing at his face.

"I'd better go home," she said at last.

He sighed, then turned the key, pushed the starter button, switched on the lights, and backed the car out of the clearing. He gunned it up the embankment and onto the highway and drove quickly to Little Juarez.

"I hope you aren't angry," she said when he stopped.

He smiled wanly and said, "A goodnight kiss would make me well."

She offered her lips to him, and he kissed her. But when he tried to pull her closer, she broke the kiss and opened the door.

"Goodnight, Kevin," she said.

"Goodnight, Rosa."

He waited until she entered the house, then turned the Ford around and drove home.

Three

The heat climbed in waves from the three brown dirt roads winding toward the foot of Leaping Panther Mountain between irregularly spaced adobe houses and brown, vacant pastures. The palisades, standing like lumpy brown-gray soldiers in close-order drill, shimmered in the brightness. Locusts hiding in the cottonwoods and mesquite and Johnson grass chirped and whirred a hot, lazy music that Kevin had thought was the sound of the sun when he was small, as he had thought that crickets and frogs were the sound of the moon.

He considered driving the Ford up Victorio Canyon to Jasper, then decided not to. Despite the heat, he felt like walking. He stepped through the front gate and chose the road to the right that wound around the mountain's eastern tip and dead-ended at the wire fence around Old Fort Appleby. It was a mile from the Adams yard to that fence, but it was late summer and early afternoon, and no one stirred from the shade of the small adobe and cinder-block houses along the way.

Kevin climbed the padlocked wooden gate into the Old

Fort. The rush of the leaves of the huge cottonwoods that had once been the fenceposts of the soldiers' corral called him to their cool shade, but he remembered the blood-thirsty mosquitos that bred in the trash-filled water of the spring there and turned away, toward the parade ground and the barracks.

The crumbling adobe walls and tumbled gray timbers of the fort were the mummified corpse of what once had been the longed-for oasis on the long, hot trail from San Antonio to El Paso. For almost fifty years it had meant safety and rest to thousands of gaunt, restless people who kept dreaming that things were better farther on and entered Fort Appleby from one desert only to leave it for another. But now it was as dead as they, its dust disturbed only by centipedes and snakes and Carl Birdsong's cows that wandered in from the sun and lay where the colonel and his wife had made love and where the privates had played poker and told lies.

Kevin liked to go there alone. He liked to hear the wind moan through the rafters and shingles still remaining, and see the fireplaces blackened by fires where soldiers had warmed their feet and backsides nearly a hundred years before. He liked to close his eyes and call into his mind the clatter of sabers and the squeak of saddles and the soft thud of hooves on the parade ground, the band's brassy blare and the bark of the sergeant's orders, and see blue uniforms, and gray ones, and gold buttons shimmering and glittering in the sun. It all seemed so brave, so glorious. He wished he had been here then. It would have been good to be here when you could move on to some place where people hadn't yet gone if you got tired of the way things were where you were. But you couldn't do that anymore, so you stayed where you were, in the dead little town around the dead fort that people once longed to see, where

25

the liveliest beings now were the ghosts.

Kevin wandered the length of the parade ground, kicking at the weeds, and flopped down in the shade of a boulder at the foot of Leaping Panther's northern slope. Nothing was moving. Nothing among the baked and tumbled buildings of the fort, nothing on the mountain or the flat, nothing on the highway, nothing in Little Juarez on the other side. Of all the wanderers who had stumbled across this flat, this mountain, this box canyon, only he was here and alive. All the others had gone, or were dead, or hadn't come and weren't expected.

Kevin, restless, got up and wandered slowly deeper into the fort's box canyon, past the parade ground, past the officers' row, past the stone foundations of the officers' wives' kitchens, past the post hospital and the powder magazine, to the end of the canyon, where the palisades rose high on three sides. His eyes found the unmarked trail that he had always used, and he began to climb, his fingers and feet finding their familiar holds among the rocks and brush. The climb wasn't hard. Soon he was standing on Leaping Panther's long crest. He rested in the shade of a small oak. Here the breeze was cool, rustling the long dry grass that no cow had ever grazed. Far below him lay the town, bright and still. Its small buildings nestled the foot of the mountain like quail chicks seeking the protection of their mother. The vast, empty flats stretched from brown, away to pale blue, to the slightly darker blue of other mountains many miles to the south and east, mocking the town's tininess, and yet emphasizing the fact of its presence on the edge of the huge nothing. The silver-painted clock dome of the two-story courthouse, just now announcing three o'clock to the nothing, the narrow dark string of highway through the town's middle, the small cluster of stores and gas stations around the courthouse plaza, the narrower brown roads

26

worn into the earth by the habits of men and animals, the brown adobe huts of the Mexicans among the cottonwoods near Victorio Creek, the orange tile roof of the Mexican elementary school, stuccoed adobe and stone houses and porches of the Anglos on the other side of the highway, the yellow brick schoolhouse and the green football field beside it, all had about them an air of age and permanence that mocked back at the emptiness.

The view from the top of Leaping Panther always stirred a vague, melancholy longing in Kevin, a yearning to write a song or poem full of love and tragedy. He had attempted it a few times, after he got home, but his sentiments always died during his labor to get them into words on paper.

His mouth was dry. He put two pebbles on his tongue to work up the saliva and began his descent of the western end of the mountain, which sloped gradually toward the brush-choked arroyo called Catclaw Gap. From there the descent was an easy walk along the edge of the arroyo, and soon he arrived at the first dirt street and the summer cabins at the mountain's foot. They belonged to doctors and lawyers and oilmen from Odessa and El Paso, Houston and San Antonio, who came to Fort Appleby for a few weeks during the polio season and then were gone again. Lincolns and Cadillacs were parked in front of some of the cabins now, and pampered paint ponies and fancy palominos grazed in the back lots of those that housed children and young ladies.

One cabin stood closer to the mountain than the others. It belonged to a lawyer named Montoya, the only rich Mexican that Kevin had ever seen. Montoya hadn't come to Fort Appleby this summer. Kevin wondered whether Montoya was in an iron lung now. Or one of his children. San Antonio and Houston in the summertime, he imagined, were like London during the Great Plague that Eisenbarger had

27

had them read about in English III. The poor were dropping in the streets, and the rich were fleeing to Fort Appleby. In Fort Appleby, polio was considered a natural consequence of living in a city. The natives found quiet satisfaction in the annual flight of slickers to their town.

Kevin heard the squeak of the maid's rocking chair before he opened the screen door. Carmelita Hawthorne glanced up at him, then back at her newspaper. She didn't speak. Kevin flopped onto the wicker settee and pulled *I, the Jury* from under the cushion where he had hidden it. He gazed at the cover picture of the blonde shedding her blouse while Mike Hammer held her at gunpoint, but he didn't open the book. He sighed and closed his eyes, then opened them again, refusing to doze. He hated the heaviness that naps left upon him after he awoke. He turned his gaze to Carmelita. She was a good-looking woman, a little younger than his mother, about thirty-six, he guessed. Her figure was good, for a Mexican of her age, fleshy, but still firm and well-defined. He wished that she would reach up and undo the braid that she had coiled into a bun at the back of her head. He had never seen her shiny black hair down, and he longed to. Carmelita played the female lead in many of his fantasies. In his favorite, he came upon her in his room, making up his bed. They were alone in the house. She had smoothed the sheets, but had not yet spread the counterpane over them. She looked up. He reached to a hairpin in the braid and pulled it out. The braid tumbled, reaching almost to her waist. Her eyes changed. She understood. "All right, Kevin," she said. She began unbuttoning her blouse, undressing slowly for him. Throughout the long afternoon they enjoyed the flesh of each other. They had just spread the counterpane and had dressed when his mother returned and found them sitting innocently on the porch. Kevin hadn't invented the fantasy. He had heard variations of it, involving half a dozen Mexican maids, from half a dozen of his friends. All claimed that it had really happened. One or two, he hoped, hadn't lied. Carmelita's eyes flickered up and caught his gaze.

"Mother asleep?" he asked.

"No. Gone. To the grocery."

"Where's Rosa?"

Carmelita smiled.

"Just seems kind of quiet," he said.

"She's at the beauty shop."

Kevin opened the book and tried to read. Mike Hammer was about to find out whether this was the Bellamy twin with the strawberry birthmark. But Kevin was too aware of Carmelita's presence to keep his mind on the story. He sighed again, lay the book on his belly, and studied the flaking white paint on the porch ceiling.

"Who is this Nixon?" Carmelita asked.

"What?"

"This Nixon who's running with the general. Who is he?"

"A senator. From California."

"Why was he chosen?"

The yard gate slammed. She turned to peek through the dark green ivy on the screen just as Rosa opened the porch door.

"You like it, Mama?" Rosa half squatted before Carmelita, turning slowly so her mother could inspect her new poodle cut. Her high-cheekboned face resembled Carmelita's, but her red hair, freckled skin, and blue eyes were her father's.

"For a dog haircut, it looks good," Kevin said.

Rosa turned and pounced. She landed astride him on the settee and tickled him roughly under the arms. "Take it back!" she demanded, laughing at his squirming. "Take it back or I'll tickle you to death!"

"Never!"

She gouged at his ribs with her thumbs. Through their laughter they heard Carmelita's reprimand. "Rosa! Leave him alone! You're too old for that stuff!"

"He insulted me, Mama." She grinned and goosed him again, then climbed off of him and straightened her skirt. She grabbed his feet and swung them to the floor. "Move over, stupid."

Kevin sat up. "You ought to come out for football," he said. "You're strong as a mule."

"I will, if all the boys are like you. You're weak as a baby chicken."

"I was afraid I would hurt you."

"Ha! Want me to break your arm?"

"Shut up, or I'll whip you both," Carmelita said.

Rosa smiled at Kevin, signaling the end of the game. "Where you been all day?"

"Walking. In the heat of the day, when all the polio germs are out."

"Where to?"

"The Old Fort. And Leaping Panther."

"To the top?"

"Yeah."

"What's up there?"

Kevin leered. "Come up there and I'll show you."

Carmelita saw the leer. "Cut it out, Kevin."

Kevin shrugged. "Want to go for a Coke, Rosa?"

"Sure."

As they walked down the sidewalk, Carmelita rose and

peeked at them through the ivy. Kevin opened the Ford's door and held it for Rosa. Carmelita shook her head sadly. Then she smoothed her apron and went into the house. The noon dishes were still on the table. Mrs. Adams would be angry if they weren't clean when she returned.

SEPTEMBER, 1952

One

Kevin stooped and cupped his hands between Travis Grey's legs. At Kevin's *Hut! Hut!* Travis slapped the ball into his palms. Kevin faded, looking for his receiver, trying to ignore the spank of pad on pad to his left. He threw too quickly and too high. Julio Garcia spurted past the defender, lunged, pulled down the ball, then belly-slid across the wet grass under the small crystal rain flung over the midsection of the field by four rotary sprinklers.

"Don't hamstring my best runner, Kevin!" Coach Wilson yelled. "We've got the whole damn season to play yet!"

As Julio rose to trot back to the scrimmage line, the back door of the school opened. Jay Eisenbarger stepped out. He paused on the edge of the concrete porch, swinging his wooden paddle pendulum-like before him. He peered toward the field into the bright after-school sun. Then he stepped off onto the gravel and trudged up the gentle slope toward the field. The painful slowness of his pace turned Wilson's glance into a curious gaze. Eisenbarger's handmade paddle, which he wielded so vigorously as scepter, swagger stick, and scourge during his working hours, dangled by its thong from his skinny wrist. His small, pale body seemed wrung dry of its usual energy and authority. As he topped the rise and started across the running track, his shoulders slumped, and he stopped suddenly and lowered his head. Wilson went to meet him. "Jay, what's wrong?"

Eisenbarger raised his head. Tears glistened in his pale blue eyes. "Jasper Birdsong has polio."

"Well, shit." Wilson's brow wrinkled under his short

crew cut. Sweat beads glistened around the furrows in his sunburnt skin. He stared at Eisenbarger, at the tears now coursing down the principal's smooth cheeks. Tears suddenly popped into his eyes, too. He rubbed his heavy, sweaty forearm across his face, then turned back to his players. They had heard. They stood like statues. Some stared at Wilson and Eisenbarger, shocked. Some gazed down at the grass, questioning, as if they had never seen it before. Then Kevin Adams walked to the sideline and threw up. The sickening rasp of his heaving broke the spell, and the other boys broke into a hubbub of questions and curses. They crowded around the men. Wilson looked over their shoulders at Kevin and called, "You all right?" Kevin, his back to the coach, nodded and waved, then threw up again. When the contents of his stomach lay puddled at his feet, he dropped to his knees and heaved again, dryly, painfully. Wilson pushed the other boys aside and walked to the sideline. Eisenbarger followed. His paddle dangled heavily from his wrist.

Wilson squatted. "Can you talk?"

Kevin shook his head. Through his tears he gazed absently at the brown and red mess that streaked his white jersey.

"He's pretty upset," Eisenbarger said. "You better let me take him home."

"Hey, Kevin, there's nothing wrong with you except that about Jasper, is there?" Wilson asked. "You're fine otherwise, aren't you?"

Kevin nodded. The heaves subsided. He felt only empty and weak, with a sour taste in his mouth. Wilson and Eisenbarger each grabbed an arm and lifted him. "Can you walk?" Eisenbarger asked.

Kevin nodded.

"Okay, son, go clean up and take care of yourself," Wilson said. "I'll bring your helmet."

Kevin nodded.

"Jay, what do you think?" Wilson asked. "Should I turn the other boys loose, too?"

"Go ahead with what you're doing. It's bad, but we mustn't make it worse."

"You don't think it would be . . . harmful?"

"God only knows, George. Do what you think is best."

"I guess I'll keep them. Take care of yourself, Kevin." He patted the boy on the rear and trotted back to where the players were waiting, quietly now, watching, gold helmets clasped like baskets in their arms. "Awright, Sanger, you take Adams's place!"

Kevin, trudging down the hill toward the gym, gently withdrew his arm from Eisenbarger's grasp. "I'm okay," he said. "You don't have to go with me."

"I'd like to, if you don't mind."

They entered the dark corridor. Kevin's cleats rattled on the concrete floor. It was a noise he usually enjoyed, but barely noticed now. With Eisenbarger's help, he tugged the soiled jersey over his head and, entering the sweat-scented locker room, hurled it through the open door of his locker. Eisenbarger sat down on the long bench. He tapped his paddle lightly on the floor while Kevin stripped and stepped into the shower.

Kevin turned it on cold, and recoiled as the needles of water shocked his sweaty skin. He inched his way back into the cold stream, determined not to reach for the hot-water handle. When his lanky body was fully within the spray, he inhaled and exhaled deeply once, then opened his mouth to the water, letting the tiny jets scour out the sour vomit taste. He glanced at Eisenbarger, sitting silently at the far end of the bench, tapping his paddle on the floor, then lowered his head into the stream, immersing all his senses in its cold.

Eisenbarger watched as Kevin turned off the water without soaping or scrubbing, stepped out onto the concrete floor again, and reached for a fluffy white towel from the stack at the other end of the bench. He was surprised at how slender the boy was, how pale and vulnerable. He wanted to say something, something silly, like, "How much do you weigh?" Something to break the shell of silence. But he didn't.

Kevin rubbed himself briskly with the towel, then fished his white shorts from under the football gear in his locker and put them on. He struggled into his long-sleeved western shirt, dark blue with tiny stripes of red and yellow, and snapped the mother-of-pearl snaps, three on each cuff and six down the front, then worked the tight Levis up his legs and around his small hips, buttoned them, and fastened the big silver buckle on the wide belt. He sat down on the bench, beside the stack of towels, and pulled on his white socks, then his maroon Juarez boots with the fancy green-and-gold stitching. Eisenbarger knew that Kevin wouldn't have bought the boots, had it not been for that stitching. He was always amused at the loyalty of the children to their school colors.

Kevin glanced at Eisenbarger and nodded. Eisenbarger rose and led the way out of the locker room, down the dark corridor, to the sun-brilliant schoolground. They paused while Eisenbarger clipped on his sunglasses, then walked slowly toward the schoolhouse. At Clay Sanger's *Hut! Hut!* Kevin peered toward the field, and saw Julio Garcia spurt through the line. Sanger's pass wobbled and fell short. Julio spat, then trotted toward the huddle.

They walked around the building and through the turnstile gate to Eisenbarger's blue Studebaker. Except for Wilson's gray Ford, it was the only car in front of the school. Kevin climbed into the front seat. The plastic seatcovers were hot against him, but Eisenbarger had left the windows down, and a slight breeze moved through them.

Eisenbarger quickly drove the three blocks to Kevin's house, raising a cloud of adobe dust behind them. He stopped, and kept the engine running while Kevin opened the door. Kevin lifted one leg out, then turned and looked at Eisenbarger. A few drops of water still clung to the boy's sandy crew cut. A small pimple glowed angry red beside his nose.

"Where *is* Jasper?" he asked.

"Abilene. Hendricks Memorial. They took him there yesterday."

"Then there isn't any doubt . . ."

"No. He's really got it, Kevin. He's got it bad."

"Well . . ." Kevin moved his lips slightly, as if trying to find words, then tears welled into his eyes. "Thanks for the ride." He stepped out and slammed the door.

The house was quiet. Mary Beth Adams was lying on the sofa in the living room, her arm flung across her eyes.

"Kevin?"

"Mother . . ."

"I know! Oh, I know!" she cried. She sat upright and reached for her son.

He knelt before her, and buried his face in her bosom and wept.

He couldn't sleep. He got up and fished his cigarettes and matches from behind the books on the top shelf of his bookcase, where he hid them from Mary Beth. He knew the screen door squeaked, so he eased it open just enough to squeeze through to the little side porch outside his room.

The match flared startlingly when he lit his cigarette. He waved it out quickly. The cigarette's orange glow and its smoke in his lungs comforted him. He sat down on the warm concrete slab and leaned his bare back against the rough stucco wall.

The lacy shadow of the mimosa tree fluttered in the silver-blue moonlight, the cool breeze barely whispering in the delicate leaves. He tried to concentrate on the breeze, moving so gently over his bare torso and legs, caressing him, relaxing him. Each time the image of Jasper in an iron lung floated into his mind, he forced it out with some brighter image of football, of sex, of travel, long travel in a Cadillac or Jaguar across the deserts surrounding Fort Appleby's oasis to some bright-lit city of adventure. But for years his best adventures had been shared with Jasper, and his attempt to exclude his friend from his fantasies made him feel guilty and afraid.

As the courthouse clock struck midnight, Kevin pushed himself up from the concrete and crept back into the house. He dressed quickly and tiptoed back to the porch and around the corner of the house to Jasper's car. He opened the door and slipped in, thankful that the dome light didn't work. He fished in his pocket for the key and started the engine, gritting his teeth at the noise. He U-turned into the street and drove slowly toward town. He stopped at the courthouse plaza, debated whether to turn right or left, then, for no particular reason, turned left and drifted in second gear up the narrow highway, Fort Appleby's only business street. Dim bulbs burned in a few of the small adobe and stone store buildings and gas stations, but most were dark. The old-fashioned streetlights, extending like gallows from wooden poles at irregular intervals along the highway, illuminated only small spots on the pavement.

Soon Kevin had passed the last gas station and the looming bulk of Leaping Panther's paws and head. The ruins of Old Fort Appleby sprawled in the moonlit canyon, and ahead, along the creek bank, among the cottonwoods, lay Little Juarez, its small houses invisible in the shadows of the trees and Star Mountain behind them, except where a single light burned. Kevin turned onto the dirt road and drove slowly toward the light. It was at Carmelita's house. He stopped and cut the engine. Casting about in his mind for a reason for what he was doing, he passed through the yard gate and knocked on the screen door. The house was open. He heard a stirring in the rear, then the whisper of bare feet on linoleum.

"Kevin! What's the matter?" Carmelita asked from behind the screen.

"Nothing. I came to see Rosa."

Carmelita hesitated. Kevin knew her eyes were questioning him, although he couldn't see them. Then she said, "Come in." She unhooked the latch and walked back through the small living room to the kitchen, where the light was. He followed her. She waved him to a white breakfast chair at the little table.

"Do you want some coffee? It's made already." Her red seersucker robe was buttoned with little white buttons from hem to throat. When she reached into the cabinet for cups, her calves flexed, brown and strong. Her hair lay wide and flat across her shoulders, almost to her waist. When she poured, the steam and aroma of strong coffee made Kevin sweat.

"Did you hear about Jasper?" he asked.

"Yes. I couldn't sleep." She turned, holding the cups, and looked at him solemnly. "Do you want to talk about it?"

"No. I came to see Rosa."

She placed the cups on the table and sat down beside

41

him. She reached into his shirt pocket for his cigarettes and lit one. "Why?"

"I want to talk to her."

"What about?" She watched him carefully through the curling blue smoke.

"About . . . things."

"She isn't here. Old Maria Gallego is sick. I sent her over to stay with her."

"Oh." Kevin lit a cigarette, too, and lifted his cup, avoiding her eyes.

"It's late, isn't it?" she said quietly.

"Yes. After midnight."

"A funny time for talking."

"I was just driving by and saw your light."

"Umm." She sucked on the cigarette, squinting through its smoke. They fell silent. Kevin concentrated on the white hairbrush on the table, averting his eyes from it only when he lifted the cup to his lips. She ground out her cigarette butt in the glass ashtray, reached for Kevin's pack, and lit another. "Kevin, do you mind if I ask you a question?"

"No."

"Are you in love with Rosa?"

Kevin's hand trembled. He set the cup down on its saucer and glanced at her, then back at the hairbrush. "I . . . ."

"You don't have to answer if you don't want to."

"No, no, I don't mind telling you. I . . . Yes. I guess I'm in love with her." He raised his eyes and returned her steady gaze. She revealed no emotion at all. Only interest.

"Would you like to date her?"

"Yes."

"Do you intend to?"

"As a matter of fact, yes. I . . . ."

"Oh, damn, Kevin! Don't you know what that would do? It would be a *scandal!* The whole town would . . . ."

"Well, damn it, I don't care!"

"You don't care!" Carmelita's body was tense. Her dark eyes flashed. "My silly daughter doesn't care, either! But Carmelita cares! Mrs. Adams will care, if she finds out! Oh, yes, *we* care, Kevin! The widow women care!" Her voice was honed to a sharp, jagged edge. "We've lived here a long time. We *care!* We've seen it happen. It's not a happy business, Kevin, this falling in love of *gringos*—Anglos— with Mexicans."

"Oh, for Christ sake, Carmelita! The Hawthornes—"

"The Hawthornes are *Mexicans*. They have been ever since old Dietrich married one. You know that! Every Hawthorne man since then has married one of us!" She lowered her voice almost to a whisper. "Blood doesn't matter, Kevin. It's what people think!"

"So what? Even if I wanted to date Helen Garcia or Cora Aguilar, what difference would it make? It doesn't make sense . . ."

"Ah!" Carmelita smiled slightly and tapped her forehead with her finger. "A *thinking* man! A man of *brain*, eh? Well, brain doesn't tell the world how to run." The smile faded. "I forbid you to go anywhere with Rosa alone."

Kevin shrugged. "I understand what you're saying. I don't want to fight with you about it."

"No. You won't fight. You'll just sneak her up to Victorio Canyon in the dark. No picture shows. No hamburgers. No nothing. Just Victorio Canyon in the dark. You've already done that."

Kevin's head jerked up.

"No, she didn't tell me," Carmelita said. "I saw you. I thought it was Jasper until I saw his car at your house the next morning."

Kevin stared into his cup. Carmelita grasped his chin in her palm, lifted it, and turned his face toward her.

"Love my daughter, Kevin," she said softly, "but love her like a sister. Life is hard enough." She dropped her hand, and Kevin stared into the cup again.

"Did you make love?"

"What?"

"Did you *fuck* her, Kevin?"

"No."

"Did you want to?"

"Yes! But I didn't. I didn't try. I wouldn't do *that!"*

Carmelita nodded, a sad little smile played around the corners of her mouth. "You're a good boy, Kevin. But someday you would try, and she would let you."

Kevin would say nothing. Carmelita gazed at his bowed profile, curiously at first, then sadly. "You're very restless, aren't you?" she said.

"Yes."

"And lonely."

He nodded.

She stood and laid her hand on his shoulder. "I'm sorry. I'll be right back. We'll talk about something else." She padded into the living room. She hadn't been gone long when she called, "Kevin, come in here, please."

The living room was still dark, but a thin line of light glowed under a door to his right.

"In here," she called.

A small lamp was burning on the dresser. She was lying on her back on the snowy sheet, her legs slightly bent, slightly apart, her hair fanned out around her head, over the pillow. One hand rested quietly on her belly. She raised the other, beckoning, and smiled.

He stood at the foot of the iron bed and undressed, never moving his eyes from her shadowy face, her wide hips, her beckoning hand.

"Love my daughter like a sister only," she said softly.

"Yes."

"Promise?"

"Yes."

He came to her and kissed her once long upon the lips, then entered her. Her warm, moist body clutched at him, then clung to him, then enveloped him, slowly, totally.

"Oh, yes. Oh, yes," she whispered.

"Yes," he said.

Two

In 1854, a young, redheaded man named Anton Dietrich left his native Antwerp and sailed for America. He landed at Galveston, and the first person he met was an Army recruiter.

"Do you speak English?" the recruiter asked.

Anton, puzzled, shook his head.

"What's your name?" the recruiter asked. He had taken some papers out of the pocket of his blue uniform coat, and was writing.

"Anton Dietrich."

"Dietrich?"

Anton nodded.

"Dietrich what?"

Anton didn't understand. He shrugged. The recruiter at that time was struggling through the third book he had read in his life. It was in his pocket. He pulled it out to serve as a makeshift desk for the papers on which he was writing. It was *The Scarlet Letter*.

"Hawthorne," the recruiter said. "You are Dietrich Hawthorne."

Anton nodded, and the recruiter wrote on the paper.

Dietrich Hawthorne marched westward with the infantry

and helped build Fort Appleby. The post was supposed to protect the settlers moving over the southern route of the Overland Trail, but even an ignorant immigrant could see the futility of it. Infantry, struggling over these rough mountains, thirsty and footsore, pretending to pursue Apaches on horseback.

Dietrich made friends with the sutler at Fort Appleby, a Mexican named Rafael Rodriguez. When Dietrich's hitch was up, Rafael turned the sutler's store over to someone else, and the two friends built a house in the canyon that later would be called Victorio Canyon. Cavalry replaced the infantry, and the two men rounded up mustangs and broke them and sold them at the fort. When the stage line was established, their house became a way station, and they provided horses for the stages, too. Rafael became a driver. Dietrich ran the station. They bought some cattle, provided beef for the Army, and made some money.

Then the war broke out in the East. The bluecoat soldiers left, the graycoat soldiers rode in, stayed a few weeks, and rode out again. Nicholas was chief of the Apaches. From time to time, he would ride into the canyon and drive off a cow to feed his braves, and Dietrich never raised a hand against him. Even when Nicholas made off with the mail company's horses, Dietrich made only a pretense of tracking him and rode back to the stage station emptyhanded, knowing he would have to face Rafael's wrath in only two or three days. Rafael stomped around the small room for two hours, railing and blaspheming, pointing his finger at Dietrich in the presence of two grinning passengers, who took advantage of the turmoil to deplete Dietrich's liquor supply without paying. But when Rafael finally climbed the box and whipped his tired horses on toward Barrel Springs, Dietrich still held no grudge against Nicholas. Indians, even Apaches, were human beings, he had believed, even in the days when he was a soldier. They tired when they rode a long way. Their bellies hurt when they were hungry. Why should they be punished for doing what any white man would do if he were tired or hungry and had the chance to steal what he needed? Hadn't Nicholas himself eaten peppers and *frijoles* at Dietrich's table? Hadn't Nicholas called him friend?

The day Dietrich removed his hat and peered carefully over the parapet of the chapel roof at all the fires on the parade ground, he was angry at Nicholas. A hundred warriors were out there, he figured, most of them gathered around the fires. The aroma of cooking beef raised a knot in Dietrich's belly. His beef. All of his beef. And their supper. The loss of his meat to Nicholas was more offensive to him because it was being consumed in his sight. He wondered what would happen if he lowered the ladder and climbed down, walked across the parade ground to Nicholas's fire, and extended his hand. Was Nicholas out to kill, or just celebrating the departure of the soldiers?

If Dietrich had been alone, he would have lowered the ladder. But there were others to consider. Two women were mixing flour and water in a shallow wooden bowl over by the wounded man. They crouched low. Hungry as he was, Dietrich didn't look forward to eating raw dough. He wished he had had the foresight to throw a few sticks of firewood into the wagon with the barrel of water, the sack of flour, and the wounded man when he fled to the fort. He wouldn't have been so careless had it not been for the wounded man. It had appeared that the Apaches might really be in a killing mood, and when Dietrich was a soldier, he had seen what they sometimes did to captives. He had never dreamed that Nicholas would camp on the parade ground.

The wounded man's friend had urged him not to rein in

when they met the two women on the road. But Dietrich couldn't bear the thought of two women, walking alone, suddenly encountering Nicholas and a hundred braves. He had reined in, and was surprised that he didn't know the walkers. They were dressed in black, and the elderly one clutched a small black book in her plump hand, although there was no longer any church at Fort Appleby or the tiny abandoned village around it. They climbed aboard quickly when he told them of their danger.

"Quién está usted?" he had asked the plump one as she seated herself beside him and shook the dust from her long skirt.

"Peregrinas," she said. Pilgrims. Dietrich had opened his mouth to ask whether the word signified their name or their activity, then he only shrugged. What did it matter? He knew of what little importance names could be.

The younger woman was quite small, hardly more than a child. She was dark-skinned, like her companion, and her black hair fell in two braids over her shoulders. Her features were delicate and bony.

The wounded man had lain still and silent for some time now. Dietrich hoped he wasn't dead. He never could bear the sight of death. And if the Apaches decided to remain on the parade ground for long, his stench would drive the refugees into Nicholas's arms. The wounded man's companion had said his friend caught the bullet near Eagle Rock, just after the Apaches spotted them. The companion was a young man, a large, squarely built man. He had a funny, Indian-sounding name. Birdsong. He looked like an Indian, too. Very dark. As dark as the two women.

The men were deserters, maybe, from one army or the other. Others had come by Dietrich's house before, on their way to the Rio Grande or the wilderness of the Big Bend. Dietrich would never ask them, and they would never

48

tell him. He wondered if he would be dead now if they hadn't shown up at his door. Or would Nicholas have come, stolen a few cattle, and gone his way? The Apaches had arrived at the fort less than an hour after Dietrich had found the ladder propped against the chapel wall, hustled the women up it, helped Birdsong struggle with the wounded man and the water barrel, unhitched and unharnessed the mules, whipped them away, and carried their harness up the ladder with him.

Dietrich had seen Nicholas point toward the empty Army corrals, and several of his braves had driven Dietrich's cattle there and penned them. One of the braves had plunged a knife into a young steer's throat immediately, and the animal's hideous bellow had frightened the women. The plump one had squealed softly and crossed herself. Similar bellows of fear and surprise had issued from the corrals from time to time throughout the night and the following day, while the braves lounged around the fires, cooking and eating. Occasionally a couple would rise and wrestle, and the laughter of the spectators drifted across the parade ground to the chapel roof. Wood crews battered down the doors of officers' quarters and barracks, disappeared into the buildings and emerged with mantelpieces, barrels, doors, a few pieces of furniture, even floorboards, to feed the fires.

The young woman crawled awkwardly to Dietrich on all fours, clutching a large wad of raw bread in one hand. "It's time to eat," she said.

"You speak English, then?" he asked.

"Yes."

Dietrich sighed and smiled. As embarrassed as he was by his English, it was eloquent compared to his Spanish. "What is your name, then?" he asked.

"Maria."

Dietrich nodded. "I am Dietrich," he said.

She pressed the wad of dough into a kind of cake and offered it to him. "Eat."

He tore off a piece and tried to chew. It stuck to his teeth.

"Do you want water?" she asked.

He glanced toward the water barrel. The wounded man was awake, and the plump woman was cradling his head, pouring water into his mouth from one of Birdsong's canteens.

"No. I'll get it later. I am from Belgium."

"Yes," she said.

"Do you know where Belgium is?"

"No."

Dietrich smiled. She was even more shy than he. He liked talking to her. "Where are you from?"

She pointed in the direction of the abandoned village.

"Why do I not know you?"

She shrugged. "I've heard of you."

"Why didn't you go to Presidio with the others?"

"My uncle was sick."

"Where is he now?"

"Dead."

Dietrich nodded toward the plump woman. "Is she your uncle's woman?"

"Yes."

"You were walking to his grave, then."

"No. A long time ago, he built a small shrine to Our Lady in the canyon. We were walking there. We didn't know about the Indians."

Dietrich nodded. "I've seen the place. It's very beautiful." He stuck the last morsel of dough into his mouth and licked his fingers. "This is very good."

Maria giggled. The plump woman, seated now across the chapel with her back against the parapet, raised her head

50

from sleep or prayer, glanced at them, then lowered it again. "It is *not* good," Maria said. "It's terrible."

Dietrich laughed. "You're right. But I've eaten worse."

"We mustn't laugh. The Apaches might hear us."

"They won't. They're eating, and they've posted no guards."

"Will they kill us?"

"I don't think so. I think they're just having a good time, because the soldiers have gone."

"They shot him, didn't they?" She pointed toward the wounded man.

"They told me so."

"Then why won't they kill us?"

"I don't think they will."

"Then why are we hiding here?"

"Because I don't know for sure."

"Who is he?" She pointed toward the wounded man's friend.

"His name is Birdsong."

"Is he a good man?"

"I know his name. Nothing else."

"It's a strange name."

"Yes."

"I'm afraid of him."

"It's because you don't know him."

"Yes. Are you a good man, then?"

"I've been told that I am."

They remained on the roof for two more days, then Nicholas and his braves went away, driving the remainder of Dietrich and Rafael's cattle before them. The wounded man was dead. Dietrich and Birdsong buried him in the cemetery at the fort, then Birdsong found his horse watering at the creek, caught it, and rode away. Dietrich and the two women walked up the canyon to Dietrich's house. The

51

Indians hadn't harmed it. By the time Rafael arrived and turned his weary coach horses into the corral, Dietrich had slept with Maria for four nights and considered her his wife.

The war ended, the soldiers came back, and Dietrich and Rafael helped them rebuild the fort. They reestablished their herd. Victorio, who was now chief of the Apaches, was killed in Mexico, and his braves were driven to a reservation in New Mexico. Dietrich and Rafael prospered. Rafael, up in years, married and built a house in town. He sired a son, Eduardo. All the offspring of Dietrich and Maria died as children, save one son of Dietrich's old age.

The boy, Gregorio, was standing beside his father in the doorway when Jason Birdsong rode up with the sheriff and the paper from the lawyer. Dietrich and Rafael had never filed the proper papers, the sheriff said. The land belonged to Birdsong now. Behind the graying beard, Dietrich recognized the young man from years ago on the chapel roof. If Birdsong recognized Dietrich, he didn't acknowledge it.

Rafael remained in town, and didn't come to the ranch again. Dietrich stayed on the ranch and worked for Jason Birdsong. He never mentioned the chapel roof. Gregorio stayed on the ranch, too, and worked for Jason's son, Wallace Birdsong. And when Wallace was thrown from a horse and broke his neck, Gregorio worked for Wallace's son, Carl. So did Gregorio's elder son, Felipe, until he was wounded in the war against the Japanese and whiskey killed his shot-up guts, leaving Carmelita a young widow with a small daughter. So did Gregorio's younger son, Emiliano.

Jimmy George Duncan, foreman of Carl Birdsong's Circle-B ranch, drove Emiliano to Hendricks Memorial Hospital in Mrs. Birdsong's powder-blue Cadillac. Mr. and Mrs. Birdsong were at Hendricks already, and Jimmy George didn't think they would mind his using the car.

Old Gregorio went along. It was the first time he had ever ridden in a Cadillac. He was amazed at its speed.

Three

Jay Eisenbarger loosened his tie and unbuttoned his collar. He turned on the fan and glanced at the stack of yellow cards on his desk. In Houston, they had women to do the clerical work. But in Houston, they had other people to teach Beowulf and Shakespeare and Hawthorne and Twain, too. He was a teacher. Four years as assistant principal in a Houston kid factory had taught him that. Even the Mexican kids at Fort Appleby High liked to hear him talk about "Wild Bill Shackspur," and "Buckle-Shoe Puritan" Hawthorne and Beowulf "The Chopper," and "Steamboat" Clemens. Some of them even read the books.

He flipped on the radio as Lefty Frizzell's nasal twang and whining steel guitar were fading and Kyle Kimbrow began his daily stumble through the Mrs. Smith's Bread commercial. Eisenbarger listened carefully. Kimbrow goofed one day and told Eisenbarger: "Get the breast in bed! Get Mrs. Smith's!" Now Eisenbarger closed his eyes every time he heard the commercial and dreamed of Mrs. Smith. Sometimes she was Marilyn Monroe, sometimes Rita Hayworth. She always lay naked on black satin sheets, smiling, cupping huge, red-nippled breasts in her palms, offering them to Eisenbarger. Today she was Rita Hayworth. "Get the best in bread! Get Mrs. Smith's!" Kimbrow said. Rita's smooth shell cracked like an egg and fell away, revealing a wrinkled grandmother, gray hair piled upon her head, leaning over a rolling pin. "Go to hell, Kimbrow," Eisenbarger said.

"And now the news. Fort Appleby, a town that never experienced a case of polio until this week, has reported its second case. The new victim is Emiliano Hawthorne, a seventeen-year-old ranch hand. Hawthorne was employed on the Circle-B ranch, northwest of the town. Fort Appleby's first polio victim, Jasper Birdsong, is the son of Carl Birdsong, the owner of the ranch. Last year, young Birdsong was an all-district halfback on Fort Appleby's regional championship six-man football team. Hawthorne and Birdsong are still the only polio victims reported in the mountain area so far this year. Other regions have not been so fortunate, though. The U.S. Public Health Service announced today that three thousand five hundred and fifty-nine cases of polio were reported in the country for the week ended August thirtieth. That number does not include the two Fort Appleby cases . . ."

"Go to hell," Eisenbarger said. He hated KQLB. He hated Kyle Kimbrow and Lefty Frizzell. He hated Sharon for harboring them, and hated Fort Appleby for its isolation. He hated Beethoven, Bach, and Mozart for their failure to be loved in West Texas, hated newscasts, hated his father for addicting him to them, hated Genevieve's asthma for forcing them out of pestilent, cosmopolitan Houston to a wasteland where the likes of Frizzell and Kimbrow held sway.

"This total, according to the National Foundation for Infantile Paralysis, set a new record for any week in the nation's history," Kimbrow droned. "About a third of the cases reported occurred in Texas, with Houston leading the pack of the Lone Star State's urban centers . . ."

Leading the pack. Rah! Rah! Houston! Fighting for its umpteenth State Polio Championship. Eisenbarger hated Kimbrow.

". . . precautions against polio. Keep clean, avoid chilling

54

and fatigue . . ." Eisenbarger moved his lips in unison with Kimbrow. He knew them all. ". . . keep children with their own friends, and watch for early signs of sickness. Severe headaches, fever, sore throat, sore muscles, dizziness . . ."

He remembered the look in Jerry Gardner's eyes that steamy afternoon he had run across the street and asked Eisenbarger to drive them to the hospital. Fear. No, panic. And grief. He remembered the braces in the Gardners' Christmas-card photograph last year. The steel reflected the flashbulb. She was smiling, though. Cute little thing. Blonde. "Only a slight limp, eventually, thank God . . ." Jerry had scrawled on the back. Eisenbarger had thought of her many times since Ginnie was born. How old? Let's see . . . Ginnie's two, we moved here . . . my God, six! Six years old. Starting to school.

"And in Korea . . ."

Eisenbarger switched off the radio. He screwed the top off his Thermos and poured the black coffee. It was morning coffee, only lukewarm now. Was his father right? Did hot coffee really cool the body on a hot day better than something cold would? "Equalizes the temperature inside and out," he used to say. "Puts you in tune with your environment." He smiled. The original John Jay Eisenbarger.

Eisenbarger pulled the stack of yellow cards toward him and flipped through them, comparing the names on them to the lists drawn from the school census cards the parents filled out last spring. He made a small red pencil mark beside the name of each child on the list who hadn't enrolled so far, drawing through the names of two who had moved. He started to draw through Jasper Birdsong's name, then didn't. He finished quickly, reached for the telephone, and cranked it.

"Number, please."

Eisenbarger recognized the gravelly, manish voice. "Hi, Amy. How's Southwestern Bell this afternoon?"

"Southwestern Bell's ears are tired. How are you, Mr. Jay? Checking the absentees?"

"Yes."

"Fire away, Mr. Jay."

"Let's see. Ring me Rogelio Andreas. That's the Lazy R, isn't it?"

"Rogelio works for Lucky Seven now. They don't have a phone out there."

"Oh. I'll write him a letter."

"Rogelio can't read, Mr. Jay."

"Okay, I'll write it to Jim and let *him* read it to Rogelio. Jim knows those kids are supposed to be in school."

"Hold on, Mr. Jay. Somebody's ringing. Be right back."

Eisenbarger sipped the coffee and glanced at the big pendulum clock on the wall above his desk. Twenty minutes after three. He smiled. He would get home early.

"That was Jean Ellis, calling her mother," Amy said. "Who's next, Mr. Jay?" She sounded bored.

"Is anybody at the Birdsong house today?"

"Haven't had a call in or out of there all day. I guess they're all in Abilene. Want to try the ranch?"

"Please."

Amy rang several times. There was no answer.

"I guess Jimmy George is still in Abilene, too," Amy said. "He's usually getting up from his nap now. What do you think it is, Mr. Jay?"

"What's that, Amy?"

"What's causing that polio out there? First Jasper, and now Emmy."

"I wish I knew. I wish *somebody* knew."

"It gives me the creeps. It's like the judgment of God. It really is. Straight out of the blue."

56

"Nobody knows much about it, I guess."

"You know what this town better do, Mr. Jay? You know what it better do right now? Tonight?"

"What's that, Amy?"

"Get down on its knees and pray, that's what. Long and hard. God will not be mocked. That's what the Bible says."

"Amy, get me Carmen Herrera, will you?"

Eisenbarger completed his calls quickly, then placed the phone on its cradle. Eduardo Rodriguez was standing in the doorway.

"What is it?"

Eduardo gestured toward the chair beside Eisenbarger's desk. His hand trembled.

"Sit down, Eduardo. What is it?"

Eduardo perched on the edge of the chair. He rested his elbows on his knees and kneaded his face between his hands. He mumbled something.

"What?"

Eduardo raised his head. "Juanito."

"Juanito? Your grandson?" Eisenbarger leaned over the desk toward the old man, his head cocked, squinting.

Eduardo nodded. "Gilberto and Ernestina took him to Sharon today, to the doctor . . ." The old man gnashed his teeth. His breath whistled softly.

Eisenbarger's palms were sweating. He wiped them on his trousers legs. "The doctor sent them to Abilene," he said quietly.

Eduardo nodded.

Eisenbarger walked around the desk and put his arm around the old man's shoulders. "I'm sorry," he said. "I'm so sorry."

Eduardo didn't answer, and Eisenbarger could think of nothing else to say. He stood with his arm around Eduardo's shoulders, patting him gently. The clock ticked.

The fan whirred. The voice of George Wilson yelling at his boys floated through the open window. Eisenbarger patted Eduardo's shoulder. The old man stirred.

"If there's anything I can do . . ." Eisenbarger said.

"Dolores and I, we're going tonight, on the bus."

"Of course. Do you need a ride to Sharon? I'll be glad to . . ."

"No, sir. We have a ride. Thank you. But you need somebody . . ." Eduardo gestured vaguely.

"Don't worry, Eduardo. We'll get somebody."

"Felix Torres. He knows where things are. He knows what to do."

"Yes. I'll get Felix. Don't worry, Eduardo. Go home. You've got things to do."

Eduardo picked a scrap of paper off of the floor. He wadded it and pitched it into the trash basket beside the desk. He rose and gazed absently around the office. "Thank you," he said. He pointed toward the door. "My broom . . ." Then he shuffled out.

Eisenbarger sat staring at the red pencil on the green desk blotter. He tried to think, but could think of nothing to think. So he stared, listening to the clock tick and the fan whirr and Wilson's voice through the window. After a long time, he got up and turned off the fan and put on his coat. He picked up the red pencil and put it in his breast pocket.

When he closed the front door, Coach Wilson's boys were lying in a circle at the north end of the field, straining at leg-lifts. "Travis!" Wilson yelled. "Don't let 'em down till I tell you! Awright, now! *Three!*"

Eisenbarger stopped to clip on his sunglasses. "Hey, Jay!" Wilson yelled. "Any news from Jasper?"

Eisenbarger cupped his hands to his mouth, intending to shout about Juanito. "No!" he yelled.

Genevieve met him at the door with a cup of coffee. "I

heard. It's the first one in town, isn't it?"

He nodded and kissed her on the cheek. He set the coffee cup on the end table by the sofa and took off his coat. "Where's Ginnie?" He sat down and propped his feet on the coffee table, then heard the bang of the toilet lid and smiled. "How's the project going?"

"Wait." Genevieve rushed out of the room. Eisenbarger heard her exclaiming over the marvel in the toilet bowl. Small feet pattered in the hallway.

"Da!"

"Good girl, Ginnie! Big girl! Come here, Sweetie!" he leaned and stretched out his arms. She rushed into them, and he lifted her onto his lap. He patted her plastic training pants. "Good girl!"

Genevieve returned smiling. "She really did it," she said. "She's really learning." She went to the kitchen and returned with her own cup of coffee and sat down in the platform rocker. She rested the cup on the chair's wide arm. "That little boy was kin to the janitor, wasn't he?"

"*Is* kin to the janitor. His grandson."

"They live in town, don't they?"

He nodded. "Gilberto Rodriguez's boy. The carpenter."

"Oh, yes." She leaned her head against the chair's high back and gazed at a ceiling corner of the white-plastered room. A cobweb was in the shadow. She moved her eyes to the window.

"Honey . . ." Eisenbarger said softly.

"Hmm?"

"Do you believe in the judgment of God?"

Her eyes widened. "What a question! Of course I do!" She laughed.

"Amy Ferguson says it's the judgment of God. The polio."

"Amy Ferguson is nuts. She's a fanatic. What's little old

59

Fort Appleby done to God? Or Jasper Birdsong, or whoever?"

"That's part of the game. Trying to figure out why God's mad at us."

"You're nuts, too. You never thought it was God in Houston."

"You expect things like this in Houston. The big city. It's just bigger when it happens here. Nothing ever happens here, right? So when something *does* happen, people think there has to be a reason."

"Right."

"But there *doesn't* have to be a reason. Things can happen here just as they do in Houston. Without reason."

"Right."

"That's scarier than Amy's idea."

"Oh, Jay, shut up. You're making me nervous."

"What's for supper?"

"Chili or vegetable soup. Your choice."

"No wonder I married you."

"Lucky man."

Genevieve was in a sexy mood. She wanted to go to bed as soon as Ginnie was asleep, but Eisenbarger resisted. A memory worked at his mind all evening. "You go ahead," he said. "I won't be long." At ten o'clock she went, in a huff. When Eisenbarger knew she was asleep, he pulled the Bible out of the bookcase and laid it on the coffee table. It was crazy. It was something his father had done every morning, believing the Good Book would give him an omen for the day. It was crazy. But Eisenbarger closed his eyes and opened the book. His finger moved over the open page until he decided to let it stop. He opened his eyes and read the verse that was under his finger. "He beholdeth all high things. He is a king over all the children of pride." Job. Forty-first chapter, last verse.

Eisenbarger read on into the next chapter. "Then Job answered the Lord, and said, 'I know that thou canst do every thing, and that no thought can be withholden from thee. Who is he that hideth counsel without knowledge? Therefore have I uttered that I understood not, things too wonderful for me, which I knew not. Hear, I beseech thee, and I will speak. I will demand of thee, and declare thou unto me. I have heard of thee by the hearing of the ear, but now mine eye seeth thee. Wherefore I abhor myself, and repent in dust and ashes.' "

Eisenbarger closed the book. Bullshit. It comes of listening to telephone operators. Or to the original John Jay Eisenbarger. He needed a drink. He never drank, but he needed one. He returned the Bible to the bookcase and walked to the kitchen. He pulled Genevieve's fruit-cake brandy down from the cabinet. The bottle was three or four years old, and still almost half full. He poured a jelly glass half full, set the bottle on the drainboard, and went back to the living room. He almost choked on the first swallow, but soon got the knack of sipping. The more the brandy warmed him, the better he liked it. He had poured too much. It was taking him a long time to finish, and his nose and fingertips were throbbing. He liked it. He gazed at the bookcase across the room, thinking of nothing. He smoked until the ashtray was full. When only a swallow remained, he singled out the Bible among the books and saluted it with his glass. "Hey, Job, you're full of shit." He drained the glass. "Go to hell."

He rose, and lost his balance. He grabbed the arm of the sofa, then groped his way to the bedroom. "John Jay Eisenbarger Junior, you're drunk."

61

He crawled between the sheets and snuggled against Genevieve's back. She was wearing her thin nightgown, her sexy one. He reached over her body and cupped his hand over her small breast. "Good evening, Mrs. Smith," he said. Then he fell asleep.

Four

Willie Joe Callahan hadn't always been a preacher. He grew up on a rocky, mesquite-ridden sheep ranch in the Devil's River country, and when his father died, Willie Joe and his almost new bride moved into the same small adobe hut at the end of the rocky road, twenty miles from the highway. The road wound unnecessarily, detouring boulders and large yuccas. It was carved out of the stony ground before Willie Joe was born, but he knew it had been built by Mexicans. White men would have removed the rocks and yuccas and straightened it out. He liked the hut, even though its sheet-iron roof made it an oven during the long sunlight hours, and at night the metal ticked, like an engine cooling. He liked his job, too, and never dreamed of living anywhere else. Then he hurt his hand, and old man Whitehead told him he had no use for a crippled cowboy.

That was when Willie Joe went to the revival and accepted Jesus as his personal savior and heard God calling him to preach the Gospel, all in the same wonderful night. He accepted the pulpit of Turkey Creek Baptist Church, and almost starved. Ada Lou breast-fed all their babies out of necessity. The call to Fort Appleby had been a godsend. Callahan knew, even before he preached his trial sermon there, that he would accept the job if given the chance. God was opening a way for him.

Callahan's call to Fort Appleby destroyed Kevin Adams's

faith in the power of prayer. The preacher's blood-curdling account of the eternal torments awaiting those who refused to embrace Jesus and join the Fort Appleby Baptist Church had terrified him, although he had been baptized already and believed firmly in "Once saved, always saved." Kevin prayed long and sincerely that Callahan's tiny congregation at Turkey Creek would find the extra hundred dollars a month that would make a move to Fort Appleby uneconomic. He would bow his head only reluctantly now, even when Callahan begged the intervention of the Lord on behalf of the Fort Appleby Warriors. In fact, Kevin resented the preacher's implication that the Warriors couldn't win without divine assistance. He had even threatened to quit the team last year, when Callahan persuaded George Wilson to "put Jesus in the lineup," and had prayed in the locker room before each game. He didn't quit, but his bowels became synchronized with prayer time. Kevin heard most of the prayers from the throne, and learned to time his flush to harmonize with Callahan's amen.

Kevin's surliness made no impression on the coach. Fort Appleby went undefeated and untied, and Kevin, Jasper, and Julio Garcia, the entire Warrior backfield, made the All-District team. Wilson, who before falling under Callahan's influence had attributed his team's success to the lucky green-and-gold shirt he wore to every game, wasn't about to tamper with a winning combination, especially one that included Jesus Christ.

Kevin hated everything about the preacher. His berry-red knobbiness, his sandy, oily, cowlicked hair, his ratty blue suit and brown-and-white shoes, his tacky wife whose slip was always showing, his six homely children, the hand that got caught between rope and saddle horn, his part-time job as deputy sheriff, which inspired sneers and snickers among Fort Appleby's Methodists, Presbyterians, Catholics, and Campbellites, his pinched, hard-eyed smile, his ignorance, and, most of all, his long catalogue of sins.

Sex before marriage was a sin. Masturbation, which Callahan called "the secret sin," apparently was even worse, resulting in deafness, hairy palms, and insanity. Profanity was a sin. Drinking beer, whiskey, or wine was a sin. Smoking before the age of twenty-one was a sin. Dancing was a sin. Any game requiring the use of dice or cards was a sin. Shooting pool was a sin. Picture shows, especially if seen on Sunday, were a sin. Listening to the radio on Sunday was a sin. Girls who wore shorts in public were sinners. So were women who wore bright lipstick, eye makeup, or flashy jewelry.

Callahan loved to drive the big black Ford with the siren and the red light on top, especially when he turned onto U.S. 80 and pointed it eastward down the long, straight asphalt toward Abilene. It had a special engine in it, made only for officers of the law, he had been told, and the slightest nudge on the accelerator sent it hurtling forward smoothly, like the buckskin he had ridden the day he caught his hand in the dolly and the big brindle cow smashed his knuckles between the rope and the saddle horn. The buckskin was the best horse on old man Whitehead's ranch. He started like a rocket and rode like a rocking chair. Callahan grinned, remembering the whistle of the wind in his ears and the way he used to sway so easily in the saddle, following the cuts and turns of the horse around the rocks and cacti. He had been a good rider. Jim Kermit had said that he couldn't hold a candle to Willie Joe Callahan when it came to horses, and Jim made the professional rodeo circuit for two years. "Lordy, how long ago?" Callahan thought. "That buckskin must be fifteen years old by now."

Callahan leaned forward and shifted his pistol belt with

his crippled right hand. He wore the big pearl-handled revolver on the right, cross-draw fashion, and the gun butt tended to work its way forward and get in the way of his elbow when he was driving. He never drove the black Ford unless he was wearing the gun, though, and the badge. The first thing he had done after getting the phone call was change from his preaching suit into Levis and boots and strap on "the old hog leg," as he called it.

He glanced into the rear-view mirror. The Perkins woman was looking down, her mouth tight with worry.

"How's she doing?"

The woman looked up, into the mirror. "She's asleep."

Callahan squinted at the long black string of highway shimmering ahead. "We'll be passing through Odessa. You want to stop and call somebody?"

"No."

"That *is* where you're from, ain't it? I thought you might like to stop and call your mama or something."

"Mama's dead, and Daddy took off a long time ago. There ain't nobody in Odessa that cares what's happened."

"Oh. Well . . ."

Daisy Perkins, groggy for lack of sleep, closed her eyes and thought of the big cottonwood that kept the sun off of her house trailer. Shady Rest was the nicest trailer court she had ever lived in. She loved the breeze moving through the leaves at night. The tree sounded like one of those rushing rivers she had seen in Western movies. She had always wanted to see one in person, but Permian Basin Construction & Paving never got a contract that far from Odessa. When the night wasn't too hot, Daisy liked to turn off the fan after Sam went to sleep and imagine she was lying naked on the bank of one of those rivers. She hoped Sam's crew would take its time rebuilding the road to Castalon. There were no tacky beer joints in Fort Appleby, no burned-out buildings, no trucks or oil-field machinery on the street. The stone and adobe buildings glistened under the bright sky. It looked like a picture in a magazine.

Daisy opened her eyes and gazed down at Sue Ann. She looked like a picture in a magazine, too, sleeping peacefully, the sun glinting off the tiny golden hairs on her slender legs. Seven years and three days old. She was feverish. Daisy wished she had let her buy the soldiers with her birthday money.

"I've just got these little soldiers," the storekeeper said. "I'm discontinuing toys. Too many of them get swiped."

"I like the soldiers," Sue Ann said, but Daisy didn't let her buy them. She wished now that she had. Sue Ann woke up crying that night. Her head hurt.

"How come your husband ain't with us, Mrs. Perkins?"

She jerked her head up. "Sam and some of his men took off fishing. He ain't due back till tonight. I left him a note, so he would know."

"Where'd they go?"

"Somewhere down on the Rio Grande. Down around Presidio, I think."

"They ain't likely to catch nothing down there this time of year. That river's probably dry as a bone." What Sam was likely to catch, Callahan thought, was the clap, in a two-dollar Ojinaga whore house. He shook his head. A man would drive a hundred miles for a two-dollar Mexican whore when he had this woman at home? He glanced into the mirror.

"Has your husband found Jesus?"

"What?"

"Is your husband saved?"

"Well, he was raised Church of Christ. They baptized him."

"How about you?"

66

"I was Methodist. Me and Sam got married in the Methodist Church, and went for a while. Sam started working for the road crew, though, and we started moving around all the time. When Sue Ann came along, we had a fight about whether she was going to be sprinkled or not. We just didn't talk church any more after that. Still don't."

"You wanted to sprinkle her?"

"Well, yeah. But we never did, so I guess Sam won that one."

"I don't care for Campbellites, but they're right about that. Sprinkling babies is a sin."

"I don't think much about such things. People do what their own mind is set on, I guess."

"That's just it," Callahan replied. "A baby ain't *got* his mind set on nothing. That's why it's wrong to sprinkle him before he's old enough to know what a Methodist is, even. When he grows up, he might decide he don't want nothing to do with Methodists, and he's already been made one."

"Well, I guess he could go to the Church of Christ and get himself dunked if that happened."

"Immersed."

"What?"

"Immersed. That's the *right* way of getting baptized. Not 'dunked.' Campbellites are wrong about most things, but they're right about that. If Jesus saw fit for John the Baptist to immerse him in the River Jordan, I don't see why so-called Christians have to do it any different now. That's fiddling with the Scriptures."

"Well, I'll leave that for the preachers to argue over. I don't have time for such things."

Callahan's eyes narrowed. "If I was where you are right now, I'd *start* thinking about it."

Fear flickered in Daisy's eyes. Callahan saw it. Facts are facts. No honest Christian, certainly no preacher, would hide them for the sake of being nice. "You look tuckered out," he said.

"I was up pretty near all night. You don't reckon it's really *polio,* do you?"

"I got no way of knowing. The doctors will figure it out."

"How could she get it? She ain't been in crowds, ain't been swimming, ain't been around strangers. She ain't never even seen that Birdsong boy. Or those Meskins."

"Lord knows. It comes out of nowhere, like the judgment of God." He glanced into the mirror. "Fort Appleby never had no polio till Jasper got it. It's a shame. He was one of the best backs I ever saw. A good Christian, too. His daddy's the richest man I know. The Lord works in mysterious ways, his wonders to perform."

"You think God *makes* polio?"

"Nothing happens that God don't approve of."

Daisy studied Sue Ann's face for a long time. "I don't believe that," she said softly.

Callahan shrugged. "God's either almighty or he ain't God."

Daisy's lip trembled. "You got kids?"

"Six of them."

"You going to say that if one or two or all six of them gets polio?"

"I'd pray for the strength to say it. Like Job."

"Well, good luck to *you,* preacher. If it comes to a fight between Sue Ann and God, I'll be on Sue Ann's side."

Callahan glanced at the dashboard. "We're going to need gas soon. Is it okay if I stop where I can get some coffee? I figured on a long nap this afternoon."

"Well . . ."

"I can get it to go, if you're nervous."

"I'm nervous, all right."

Callahan pulled into the left lane to pass three teen-agers

68

in a hopped-up Chevy. The driver braked suddenly when he noticed the siren and light and whip antenna mounted on the Ford, but Callahan still figured him for seventy miles an hour. He grinned at the sick look on the driver's face. "Probably got beer in the floorboard, too," he said. He waved, and the duck-tailed, bare-chested driver steered toward the shoulder before he realized that Callahan wasn't trying to stop him. "Thank your stars we ain't in Davis County, punk!" Callahan said loudly.

"It must be something, being a preacher and a deputy, too," Daisy said. "You can go to church and tell people what not to do, and then put them in jail if they do it."

"It's a special opportunity to serve the Lord, I won't deny that. The Lord loves the law, and the law serves the Lord." He gunned the car over a small rise, and the big Texaco sign of the Four Leaf Clover Truck Stop & Motel shimmered into view. "That's a pretty good place up yonder. All right if I pull in?"

"Okay."

He steered the Ford around two parked semis to the east side of the restaurant, into the shade. "Why don't you leave the child in the car and come in. We won't be long."

A burst of cold air and Slim Whitman wailing "China Doll" hit them when he opened the door. The drivers of the two semis, bent over chicken-fried steak, cream gravy, and hot biscuits, raised their heads at the door's squeak. Their eyes followed Daisy's stiff walk to the corner booth. Callahan wished she wasn't wearing such short shorts. The creases between her thighs and buttocks were visible. Truckdrivers made Callahan nervous anyway, particularly the brawny, tatooed, curly-haired kind with the aviator sunglasses and the Lucky Strikes rolled up in his T-shirt sleeve, like the man who swiveled his counter stool and grinned, even after Callahan and Daisy sat down.

69

The skinny waitress plunked down two barrel-glasses of iceless water and two handwritten menus.

"Hot out there, ain't it, Sheriff," she said.

"You can say that again, lady."

"Hot out there, ain't it, Sheriff." She giggled.

"You been out here in this sand too long, lady," Callahan said. "Why don't you tell that *hombre* at the counter that his dinner's getting cold?"

"Awright. But he'll come over and whip up on you. He's a mean one."

"Forget it, then. Just give me a cheeseburger and fries and the biggest cup of the blackest, awfullest coffee you've got."

Daisy glanced up from the menu. "I thought we were going to get coffee and go."

Callahan shrugged. "The kid's sleeping, and I'm hungry. No telling when we'll eat next."

"I'll have the same."

The cheeseburgers were big and good. But Daisy couldn't keep her eyes open. She tried to focus on the food, but couldn't. Her fingers relaxed and dropped a French fry into her lap.

"You're in a bad way, young lady," Callahan said.

"Yeah."

"I'm going to get a room."

"Hmm?"

"A couple of hours sleep will do you good. It won't hurt the girl to get some real rest, either."

Daisy squinted, trying to focus on him. "You sure?" Her eyes closed. Callahan picked up the check and walked to the cash register. The skinny waitress took his money and rang it up.

"Who do I see about getting a room?"

The waitress leered. "Me."

"Well, I want one."

"Got a prisoner you need to take care of, Sheriff?"

"One with two beds. One for me, and one for the lady and her little girl. Her *sick* little girl."

The waitress still leered. "Sure. And how long will you need it?"

"Two or three hours."

"Uh-huh. That'll be five dollars, then."

"Okay. Where do I register?"

"You don't need to register. Just give me the five."

Callahan handed her the bill, and the waitress reached to a shelf under the cash register and brought up a cigar box full of keys. "Pick one," she said. "Just leave it on the dresser when you're finished."

Callahan chose Number 4.

"That's a nice one," she said. "Close to the Coke machine."

"You're a mean, skinny bitch."

"I been out in this sand too long."

Callahan held the sleeping child against his chest. Daisy had to work the key in the lock several times before the door opened. The room stank of stale cigar smoke. "Turn on the fan," Callahan said.

Daisy did, then flopped onto one of the squeaky beds and burst into tears. "Aw, shit!" she cried. "Aw, shit."

Callahan laid Sue Ann on the other bed. He unbuckled his gun belt, took off his hat and boots, and lay down beside the weeping mother. He patted her back lightly. Her white blouse was clammy to his touch. "There," he said. "There, there."

Her face was buried in the pillow. Her shoulder trembled under his good hand. Then suddenly she turned onto her back and clasped her hands around his neck. Her blue eyes were bloodshot and wet. "I ain't had no loving in *such* a long time," she whispered.

Five

The teachers stood in the aisles, directing their pupils into seats, shushing and threatening. On the stage, Fort Appleby's tiny band, in green-and-gold uniforms, fringe along their sleeves and legs, blared "Warriors, Fight." Four cheerleaders clapped and kicked to the music. In green skirts, also fringed, and gold satin blouses and feathered headbands, they grinned slyly at the players, who were already seated in the front row. Wilson had insisted that they wear their letter jackets. They were sweating generously.

When the music stopped, Alicia Jones, the head cheerleader, stepped to the center of the stage. Jasper Birdsong's class ring hung on a thin golden chain around her neck. She cupped hands to mouth and yelled: "Who are we?"

"Appleby!"

"Who are they?"

"Henderson!"

"What we gonna do to 'em?"

"Beat 'em!"

"What?"

"Beat 'em!"

"What?"

"Beat 'em! Beat 'em! Beat 'em! Yea!"

The children screamed and whistled. Alicia smiled and waved toward the front row. Wilson rose and hitched up his pants. He wiped his hands on the front of his green-and-gold shirt and gazed into the half-filled auditorium. "I'm glad to see this fine spirit for the Warriors' first game."

"Yea!"

"The Warriors were never beaten last year. Everybody's out to get us. So come on out to the field this afternoon, and bring all this spirit with you!"

"Yea!"

Wilson paused and consulted a small index card in his palm, then gazed at the ceiling. His brow wrinkled. "I have to insert a note of seriousness here. As you know, Jasper Birdsong can't play today. He's awful sick." He halted. He swallowed. "Anyway, the boys voted to dedicate this game to him. We're going to go out and win it for him."

"Yea!"

The coach sat down. "The lineup!" somebody yelled. "The lineup!" Alicia snapped her fingers. The cheerleaders dropped to their knees.

JIM-my! JIM-my! He's our man!
If he can't do it, OS-car can!
OS-car! OS-car! He's our man!
If he can't do it, TRA-vis can!
TRA-vis! TRA-vis! He's our man!
If he can't do it, CLAY can!

Kevin Adams hated Clay Sanger's name in the lineup where Jasper's had been. "Clay can't," he thought. "Sanger can't do shit."

CLAY! CLAY! He's our man!
If he can't do it, JU-lio can!
JU-lio! JU-lio! He's our man!
If he can't do it, KE-vin can!
KE-vin! KE-vin! He's our man!
If he can't do it, NO-body can!

Alicia cut off the concluding *"Yea!"* and led the crowd into the postscript they always added to the yell before the first game of the season.

> *He's our CAP-tain!*
> *He's our STAR!*
> *He will tell us*
> *Who we ARE!*

Kevin leapt to his feet and thrust his fist toward the ceiling. *"WARRIORS!"* he screamed. It was the signal for pandemonium. The crowd whistled and stomped. Brass-players blared obscenely, drummers drummed sharply, erratically. Kevin waited for the din to subside. Then, not as loudly or cheerfully as he intended, he said, "We'll beat Fort Henderson today. We'll beat them all, like last year. But we won't do it without Jasper. Jasper won't be with us, and we'll miss him. But his spirit will be with us, just as his body has been . . ."

Kevin faltered. He sounded as if Jasper were dead. It scared him. He suddenly was aware of the faces in the audience. Some frowned attentively. Some were smiling. They were listening, waiting. "I don't think we ought to leave him out of the lineup," he said. "Let's put him back in." He opened his mouth as if to say more, then he sat down.

Alicia burst into tears and dashed offstage. Rosa Hawthorne snapped her fingers, and the remaining cheerleaders dropped to their knees.

> *JAS-per! JAS-per! He's our man!*
> *If he can't do it, NO-body can!*

Jay Eisenbarger had walked down the aisle and climbed now to the stage. He raised his hand. "I'm afraid that yell is prophetic," he said. "I've just received word that the Fort Henderson team can't come this afternoon. Fort Henderson will forfeit the game."

The audience broke into small, shocked whispers. "I'm sorry," Eisenbarger said. "Classes will continue as usual today. But have a good weekend."

"Can they do it to us, Jay? It isn't fair."

Eisenbarger rocked nervously in his swivel chair, watching Wilson pace back and forth across the small office. "Sit down, George. Let me drop the other shoe."

Wilson sat on the edge of the straight chair at the end of the desk.

"The other coaches conferred on the phone this morning, George. *None* of them is coming to Fort Appleby this season. They also requested that in view of our . . . situation . . . we not insist on playing our games scheduled in their towns."

Wilson paled. His eyes were large and hurt. "Is that . . . legal?"

"It's legal. They *all* are offering to forfeit. They'll mail you the district championship trophy right now, if you want."

"Shit! What kind of championship is that?"

"Hollow. But it's yours if you want it." Eisenbarger leaned forward, grabbed a pack of cigarettes from his desk and lit one. He blew the smoke into the face of the clock, then resumed his rocking.

"Well, shit," Wilson said. "When do I have to decide?"

"Anytime. You may accept Fort Henderson's forfeit today, and Castalon's next week, and keep on doing that until the end of the season. You may ask for the trophy, or tell them to keep it, anytime you want. Who knows? Maybe some of them will want to play you, later, if we don't have any more cases."

"It's not fair! Jasper's the only one of them that has anything to *do* with the school. Emmy hasn't been to school in a year. He's been out there on that ranch all the time . . ."

"The Birdsong ranch, don't forget."

"Yeah, but shit, that Meskin kid is just a baby . . ."

". . . Whose grandfather works at the school."

"And that little girl, I never even *heard* of her."

"None of that matters, George. You've got to look at it from *their* point of view. We're the only town in the district that's had a case of polio this year. And nearly every other area of Texas is being eaten alive. I can't blame them for being careful."

"Fort Henderson had a case last year."

"One. Late in the year."

"Bradbury had several a few years ago."

"It had two. Early in the summer, three years ago. Jesus Christ, George! Fort Appleby never had a case of polio in its history, and now we've got *four* during the first week of school. Bang! Bang! Bang! Bang! Do you know what the polio foundation calls an epidemic, George? Twenty cases for every one hundred thousand population. This town has eight hundred people and four cases of polio! That's one *hell* of an epidemic by *any*body's figuring! They're afraid their kids will *die* if they come here, George."

Wilson rubbed his eyes. "Give me a cigarette," he said. Eisenbarger tossed the pack to him, and he lit up and blew the smoke at the clock, as Eisenbarger had done. "I don't often smoke," he said.

"I know."

"Want to hear something funny, Jay?"

"I could use something funny."

Wilson's thick lips twisted into a wry grin. "This was going to be my big year. I was going to win that championship and leave this town. I was going somewhere and get me an eleven-man team."

"I knew you were thinking that way."

"Not that I don't love six-man ball. Hell, six-man's a better game than eleven-man. Faster, more exciting. But a man can't *get* anywhere in coaching without an eleven-man team. Know what I mean, Jay? Why, I've had four winning seasons and two straight championships since I came here. And who ever heard of me? Nobody. There's not a town in the district that even has a fucking newspaper. I call in our games to El Paso and San Angelo, and they won't even let me *tell* them about them. All they want is the score, and they run that in itty-bitty type. Shit. I was going to get me a job at some oil town out in the Permian Basin, where they got lots of money and big, strong boys. I've about forgotten whatever it is that tackles and guards do. I want to *see* some. I want to *coach* some. I want to make some *money*. And Fort Appleby's going to have a shitty team next year . . ."

Eisenbarger peered up at the clock. "I'm going to call a meeting of the school board," he said.

Just after two o'clock, when Kevin's typing class was uncovering its machines, Eisenbarger made the announcement. He stood near the door, swinging his paddle back and forth on its thong, reading in a formal voice from a slip of yellow paper.

"School will be dismissed at the end of the current period. All of you should go directly home. All classes will be suspended until further notice. When the Board of Education determines that the school year should resume, you will be notified. In the meantime, the board urges you to take the following precautions: Keep clean. Avoid chilling and fatigue. Avoid crowds. Avoid strangers. Do not go swimming. Watch for early signs of sickness, particularly severe headache, fever, sore throat, sore muscles, or dizziness. If any of these symptoms occurs, consult a physician. If your family does not have a car, call the Davis County Sheriff's Office, and a ride to Sharon or Bradbury will be arranged. A copy of this announcement will be given to you when you leave the room. Make sure that your parents read it, or read it to them."

Eisenbarger turned and strode out, closing the door behind him.

Rosa tossed her feathered headband into her locker and slammed the door. She dawdled at the corner by the water fountain, and watched Kevin's locker. When he appeared and put away his typing book, she stepped toward him. But Alicia grabbed him by the arm and whispered into his ear. Embarrassed, Rosa turned away. Eduardo Rodriguez was leaning on his broom in the doorway of the science lab. He called, in Spanish, "Who do you think you are, Rosa?" She ducked into the girls' rest room.

"Will you give me a ride home?" Alicia asked.

"Sure."

They were among the last to leave the school. The dust raised by those with cars hadn't settled. Clusters of walkers were still in sight along the road. Kevin stepped back to allow Alicia to pass through the turnstile gate. Her gold satin blouse and golden curls glistened in the bright sunlight.

"You sure you want me to ride with you?" she asked.

"Sure. Why not?"

She folded her arms across her small breasts. Kevin opened the car door for her. She slid across the blue plaid seatcovers.

As he pressed the starter button, she said, "I haven't seen the seatcovers."

"No, I guess not."

"How did you wind up with Jasper's car?"

"It was at my house when Jasper . . . Nobody's told me what to do with it, so I just kept it."

"Oh. He probably would have wanted you to have it, anyway."

"Jesus! Don't talk about him like he's dead!" Kevin gunned the old Ford down the dirt road, toward the highway.

"You were doing it during the pep rally. You sounded just *like* he was dead."

"I didn't mean it that way."

"That was a real nice thing, having them give that yell for him."

Kevin turned the Ford into the highway and drove past the plaza. Then he slowed to turn into the road where Alicia lived, but she touched his arm and asked, "Do you have to go home right now?"

"No."

"Let's ride up the canyon. I need to talk."

Kevin gunned the car on down the highway, past Old Fort Appleby and Little Juarez, and at the intersection took the canyon road. Alicia scooted closer to him. Her satin shoulder touched his arm.

"You heard from Jasper?" he asked.

"No. Have you?"

"No. Carmelita said they cut a hole in Emmy's throat and put a tube in it to let him breathe."

They were approaching a narrow sideroad that wound

around a cluster of huge boulders to a picnic table. Alicia pointed. "Stop," she said. "I don't want to ride. Just talk."

He pulled around to the picnic table and stopped. "God, I feel sorry for them. If that happened to me, I'd want to just go ahead and die."

Alicia stared at him, horrified. "No, Kevin!"

"Well, that's the way I feel. What would be left?"

"Jasper won't die. He's strong. Don't wish him dead. Please."

"I *don't* wish him dead! I don't wish *him* dead, I don't wish *Emmy* dead, I don't wish the others dead. I was just saying how *I* would feel, if *I* got it."

"Don't wish yourself dead, either," she said. "They must expect it to get worse."

"They don't know whether it'll get worse or not. They're just scared."

"Aren't you scared?"

"Scared shitless."

"Me, too." She laid her head on his shoulder and turned her face toward his neck. "Kiss me," she said.

Kevin pulled away.

"For Jasper. He would kiss me, if he were here. Kiss me for *him*. Please."

The soft, warm satin caressed his neck. He bent to her. Her lips parted, yielded under his. He moved to the soft, sweat-moist hollow under her ear and kissed her there, too.

"Thank you," she whispered.

It was after one A.M. when Kevin slammed the car door. Carmelita was sitting on the steps, waiting. She rose and met him at the gate. "Rosa's asleep, but we'd better stay out here," she whispered. She took his hand and led him around the side of the house. She had spread a quilt under the peach tree.

Eisenbarger awoke four times during the night. Each time, he padded into Ginnie's room and stood at the foot of her yellow crib, peering into the darkness. Each time, she was sleeping soundly.

Six

Until the schools closed, the tragedies of Fort Appleby had been small ones. Their agonies rarely extended beyond a family or two. When the federal soldiers destroyed the Confederacy and turned their attention back to the Indian tribes, the men and women who came to the deserted village and rebuilt it weren't the refugees who had fled it when the war began. Later, Apaches murdered cowboys and shepherds on isolated ranches, small parties of immigrants on the Overland Trail, and lone riders whom they surprised in their blankets and left mutilated, sometimes after hours and days of unspeakable terror and pain. Fort Appleby had buried the buzzard-picked remains, mourned and avenged them as best it could, and went on about its business. Some time after both the Indians and the soldiers were gone for good, in the 1890s, Oscar Donahue and his two almost grown daughters were drowned in a flash flood in Victorio Creek. Their bodies and the carcass of their horse and the wreckage of their buggy were found by a search party two days later, and the old men who had accompanied the party as young men still talked about it. There had been homicides and suicides, desertions, casualties of war, madness and disease, all clucked over and folded into the folklore of the town. But they were tragedies that had happened to other people, close friends or relatives or ancestors, perhaps, but other people nonetheless.

So was the polio, until the children came home carrying the yellow slips with Jay Eisenbarger's signature at the bottom. The first reaction to Jasper Birdsong's illness was surprise, and then pity. The townspeople hardly knew Juanito Rodriguez, he was so young. They barely remembered Emiliano Hawthorne, who after he quit school and the football team was just another Mexican ranch hand. They were unaware of Sue Ann Perkins's existence until Willie Joe Callahan drove her to Abilene. Their illness was unfortunate, of course, and the townspeople wished, prayed even, for their recovery. Many sent get-well cards and gifts to Hendricks Memorial. But the grief belonged to somebody else, really, for which they were thankful.

Eisenbarger's slips changed that. Suddenly the polio belonged to everybody. At first, the town was baffled. Parents read and reread the note and posted it on walls beside telephones and on refrigerator doors. But Fort Appleby people, except for a few slovenly families, had always kept reasonably clean. The town had no movie theater, no concert hall, no bowling alley, no recreational or cultural facilities of any kind, save the schools and churches, so there were few crowds to avoid, especially with the schools closed and the football season canceled. Would God strike a child in his Sunday School room? Ridiculous. There were no strangers to avoid, no swimming pool. Fatigue? Fort Appleby for a century had done little real work in the hot sun. No physician had lived in the town since the death of Dr. Bill Carter, the last of the old-fashioned horse-and-buggy physicians, almost twenty years ago. Was Fort Appleby to drive forty miles to Bradbury or twenty-five to Sharon with its every headache and sore throat?

Fort Appleby wasn't fooled by the quiet, bureaucratic tone of Eisenbarger's note. It told the town that plague was in the air, hovering in the bright sky, creeping under doors at night like a lethal fog, lurking in drinking water and toilets, befouling the breath shared during conversation and copulation. The coffee-drinkers at Martin's Drug left empty stools between them and spoke little. Mary Beth Adams and Carmelita Hawthorne and Genevieve Eisenbarger bought their groceries quickly and drove straight home. Gossip was by telephone, and always shared by Amy Ferguson, who never failed to inject warnings of judgment and Armageddon. The Women's Missionary Society and the Lions Club followed the lead of the schools and canceled their meetings. When someone asked Callahan, "What's happening to our children?" he preached on Abraham's willingness to sacrifice Isaac on Jehovah's altar. His flock wasn't comforted. Church attendance dropped. The blood of Jesus had made that kind of sacrifice unnecessary, hadn't it? The theological implications of Fort Appleby's plague had to do with Satan, not God. Maybe the town was being tested. The devout examined their souls for stains of guilt and found none.

The less religious simply worried, and were afraid. Mary Beth Adams awoke in the night and crept into Kevin's room. She stared down at his pale body, akimbo in deep sleep among the twisted sheets. She wanted to wake him and ask if he was all right. Standing in the darkness, she would remember back to his infancy and his dead father and regret that she had allowed him to grow away from her while he grew up. The young man on the bed was a stranger to her.

He was no stranger to Carmelita. Since the closing of school their lovemaking had acquired an element of frenzy that made her cry out, not always out of passion. The boy seemed determined to cram a lifetime of sex into every coupling. Her lover's intensity had pleased, even flattered her, until one night Kevin cried out Jasper's name in a fitful sleep. He awoke and entered her with a ferocity bordering on rape. Her husband, Felipe, had been that way when he returned from the war, until his shot-to-pieces guts succumbed to the whiskey. But as long as he would abide by their bargain, so would she. Kevin's aloofness bothered Rosa, she knew. Eduardo Rodriguez whispered to Carmelita of Rosa's calf eyes for Kevin, and his sensible preference for Alicia Jones. Carmelita resented the jealousy she felt. Then she would wish things were as they used to be.

"Another cup of coffee?"

"Hm?"

"You want another cup of coffee?"

"Yeah." Kevin pushed his cup toward Mary Beth, and she filled it. He was gazing into the yellow smear of fried egg on his plate.

"Having trouble waking up?"

"Just thinking."

"What about?"

Kevin's eyes flickered to her face, then away. He wished she would put on makeup before breakfast. The glisten of cold cream in the bright kitchen sunlight emphasized the deep lines around her eyes and mouth. Her gray-blonde hair looked thin when it was uncombed. Her hand, fiddling with a thread dangling from the collar of her pink chenille robe, was pale and bony. "Give me a cigarette."

"Kevin, I don't like for you to smoke."

"I'll quit when you do."

"That's not fair. I'm older."

"Just one."

The intensity of his gaze told her that he would argue. "Oh, all right. Just don't get into the habit." She snickered. "That's what the priest told the man who confessed to kissing a nun, isn't it?"

"That joke's as old as the hills." He didn't smile.

"You didn't tell me what you're thinking about."

"Jasper. I was wondering how he feels this morning." He pulled Mary Beth's Viceroys across the table and lit one with her little gilt lighter.

"I don't think the Birdsongs have called anyone since they went to Abilene. You'd think they'd get in touch with somebody."

"They've got other things to think about."

"I know, but poor Vera must have hours and hours on her hands. Carl, too. Looks like they would have called somebody. Even old Gregorio tries to write postcards. Poor Emmy. That bulbar type must be devastating."

"That's what Jasper has, too."

"I know."

Kevin set his cup down and took a long drag on the cigarette. "What does it do?"

"I don't want to think about it." She laughed harshly. "Some people! You know what Elmer Martin's doing? He wants me to sell him twenty thousand dollars' worth of life insurance on little Georgie. Can you beat that?"

"It gives me the creeps."

"You think I ought to do it?"

"Why not?"

"You really think I ought to?"

"Sure. It's Elmer who's going to cash in on Georgie, not you. Anyway, he'll let it lapse if the little fart makes it through the epidemic."

"Kevin, you're awful!"

"Well, isn't that what *you* were thinking?"

"Yes!" She laughed. Her laugh infected Kevin, and he laughed, too.

Mary Beth beamed at her son. The wrinkles around her eyes deepened. "That was nice. I haven't seen you laugh in so long. How long has it been since you laughed, huh?"

"People don't remember things like that."

"I guess not." She pulled the cigarettes back across the table and lit one, tilting her head to blow the smoke at the ceiling. "Who you working with today?"

"Mr. Jay."

"You really like him, don't you?"

"Yeah, he's okay."

The honk of the horn drifted almost musically through the shade of the living room and the long dining room to the sunlit kitchen. Kevin pushed himself away from the table. He tucked the tail of his frayed red shirt into faded, beltless Levis, then lifted his foot to the chair and tied a work shoe stained by summers of Fort Appleby lawns and Birdsong cow manure.

"Wear a hat," Mary Beth said.

She followed him to the door, clutching her robe at the throat. He grabbed a sweat-stained straw hat from the rack by the front door and pecked Mary Beth on the lips.

"If you get hot, stop and rest awhile."

"I will."

Eisenbarger in old Army khakis and a new straw hat, behind the wheel of the battered green pickup, was a parody of a ranch hand. "We've got ourselves a tall assignment," he said as Kevin banged the door shut. "Little Juarez. Lots of privies besides the trash barrels." He ground the pickup into gear and U-turned toward the plaza, glancing through the back window at the large livestock sprayer he was towing.

"Who's helping us?" Kevin asked.

"Nobody. We've got six two-man spraying crews. Everybody else is gathering water samples. This town has more wells than a dog has fleas."

"They think the water might be causing it? Everybody's *always* drunk out of his own well."

"Nobody knows what's causing it. But we've got to do something, to keep from going nuts."

An angry, metallic roar, swooping, raised the hair on Kevin's neck. "Jesus!" An ancient biplane materialized ahead of them, so low that Kevin saw the wide grin under the pilot's goggled eyes. A white plume suddenly shot from the plane's belly. It lengthened and widened into a thin cloud as the pilot flew a beeline course down the highway to Leaping Panther's paws, then veered eastward over Little Juarez.

"Cropduster!" Kevin said.

"Yeah, he and two more flew down from Pecos. Donating their time, I heard. That must be their first run. Makes you feel like a boll weevil, doesn't it?"

"Getting free help from outside means it's really bad."

"That's one way of looking at it."

"God."

Eduardo Rodriguez and Julio Garcia were in the Gulf station driveway, perched on top of a sprayer tank with the Birdsong Circle-B painted on the side. Eduardo was pouring white powder into the tank while Julio held the water hose. Julio looked up when Eisenbarger and Kevin rattled by. Kevin waved. Julio grinned and nodded.

"Why didn't *they* get Little Juarez?" Kevin asked.

"I asked for it. I've never been there. I ought to know these people better than I do."

Eisenbarger pulled off of the highway onto the dirt road that ran by the first row of small adobe houses. "Cut over behind the houses," Kevin said. "The barrels will be in the back." The tailgate chains clanked as Eisenbarger wrestled the pickup along the narrow path between the two rows of fenced backyards. Wire gates stood open along both sides of the path. "They're expecting us," Kevin said. Eisenbarger steered carefully through the first narrow gate, pulling the sprayer alongside the rusty trash barrel near the back fence. He yanked the hand brake and opened the door.

"Okay, death to the flies," he said.

Kevin wound the starter-rope around the flywheel of the sprayer's pump motor and pulled. The motor sputtered, then died. He adjusted the choke, wound again, pulled again. The motor sputtered, then caught, then faded. He moved the choke forward. The motor coughed, caught again, then climbed into a healthy roar.

"Expert," Eisenbarger said. "Make it a good, wet spray. You stay with the sprayer, and I'll drive. When you want to switch off, holler."

"Right."

Kevin unwound the black rubber hose and pulled the trigger on the big nozzle, adjusted the spray and fired it toward the trash barrel. A cloud of flies swarmed from among the fire-blackened tin cans, burnt paper and charred, stinking food scraps. Bang! You're dead! Kevin thought. An old man with a huge white mustache stood in the door of the house, behind the screen, watching him. He pointed toward the corner of the yard.

"*El tocado!*" he called.

Kevin nodded and dragged the hose to the tiny, weathered privy, half-hidden behind a huge mesquite. He soaked its gray boards, moving the nozzle up and down as if washing a car, then opened the door and shot the spray inside, letting it linger over the single hole in the wooden seat. A cloud of flies swarmed out of the hole, buzzed hysterically, dropped to the seat and the floor and kicked feebly when their wings were too wet to carry them.

"*Bueno!*" the old man called. "*Gracias!*"

"*De nada!*" Kevin replied.

They all were standing at their doors, always behind the screens. Small children clung to their mothers' dresses. The mothers and old men looked worried, as if Eisenbarger and Kevin were delivering the disease itself to their homes. Their mud dwellings were the oldest inhabited buildings in Fort Appleby. Many of them were as old as the fort itself, which was decaying and falling while roses and mimosa and children flourished in these small yards. The *gringos* hadn't brought roaring machines and foul-smelling sprays to Little Juarez before. They wanted to believe that it was necessary, and good, as the *gringos* said. At each house, Eisenbarger asked Kevin the name of the family who lived there, and Kevin was surprised at how few he knew. "You should have worked with Julio," he said.

As the morning grew warmer, and the odors of his chemicals and the trash barrels and the privies more oppressive, images of steel braces and iron lungs and wheelchairs flashed through Kevin's mind. The shiny apparatus sometimes encased Jasper and Emiliano, sometimes the children standing in the doorways, sucking their thumbs, sometimes himself. To fight off the images, he called up memories of Carmelita's body and her cries, of Rosa's laughing eyes, of the soft skin under Alicia's chin. He marveled at the abundance of womanhood open to him. How had he become such a stud so suddenly? He hadn't actually made love to Rosa or Alicia, but he was so certain that he could that he considered it done. Carmelita's arrangement with him, her fear that he was after her daughter, had convinced him that he could have Rosa if he wanted her. Alicia had almost told him outright that she wanted him to assume Jasper's place, and only his loyalty to Jasper prevented him. Carmelita confused him. He had no idea how she felt about him. She was available whenever he needed her, and she was as good in bed as he had imagined. But there was a distance between them that neither had tried to bridge. Carmelita hadn't mentioned Rosa since that first night. Carmelita and Rosa and Alicia, all naked, dancing, beckoning, moved through his mind in filmy fantasies throughout the long, hot morning of buzzing airplanes and flies, the sputtering pump, the suffocating fogs of DDT, and the maggot-infested Mexican turds. "Hey, Mr. Jay," he said at last, "I'd like to drive."

"Let's eat first. They're serving us free at the Leaping Panther today."

Kevin shut down the pump and wound the hose around the tank. He sank into the seat with a sigh.

"Tired?" Eisenbarger asked.

"No. The smells are getting to me, though."

"You can drive after lunch. We don't have much more to do, anyway, do we?"

Two of the sprayer crews were sitting at one of the Leaping Panther Cafe's small square tables, and the place reeked of DDT. The four were cowboys. Neither Eisenbarger nor Kevin knew them. They nodded as they passed the table and settled into a booth near the rear of the dark, grease-smelling room. They ordered their food and waited in silence for it. Kevin blew his nose into paper napkins several times to try to rid himself of his chemical odor. They had almost finished eating their tough roast beef and cold mashed potatoes when Eisenbarger said, "Kevin, something has been bothering me." He carefully laid his fork across his plate. He took a long draught of water and patted his lips with his napkin. He folded his hands in front of him on the table, as he did in his classroom. "I don't like to bring it up. I don't want to frighten you unduly."

"What is it?"

"Didn't you and Jasper swim quite a bit?"

Kevin tensed. "Not much. Four or five times for the whole summer, I guess."

"Where?"

"In that tank up by Jasper's house."

Eisenbarger nodded. "Did anyone else swim with you?"

"No. Well . . . somebody did once."

"Who?"

"Emmy."

Eisenbarger scooted to the end of his seat and stood up. "Let's go have a look at it."

Eisenbarger stopped the pickup where Jasper had always parked the Ford, and they crawled through the fence.

"Some of those windmills in Little Juarez are awfully close to the privies, aren't they?" Eisenbarger said.

"Yes, but nobody in Little Juarez has come down with polio."

"True."

They walked in silence then, and slowly. Kevin remembered Jasper running the last time they were here together, tearing at his clothing at the first smell of water. Kevin sniffed. He smelled only the chemicals in his nostrils. The windmill wheel was still. He pointed. "Somebody turned it off."

They walked faster. Kevin quickly climbed the makeshift ladder and peered over the rim of the tank. "It's bone dry! Somebody drained it!" He stepped to the weathered two-by-twelve where he and Jasper and Emiliano had lounged naked in the sun less than a month before. Eisenbarger climbed up and sat beside him. There were several large rocks on the tank floor. Jasper and Kevin had hauled them up and thrown them in years ago, to see them splash. Carl Birdsong had whipped Jasper for it, and had sent

Kevin home. The rocks, the floor, the wall of the tank were covered now with a thick gray coat of minerals and dry algae, curling and flaking, its deathly ugliness relieved only by the two black inner-tubes, one of them half-deflated, that lay near the far wall.

"That's too bad," Eisenbarger said. "I wanted to get a water sample."

"I never saw it dry before . . ."

"They shouldn't have drained it. Not yet."

Kevin craned his neck and peered into Eisenbarger's eyes. "Do you think this is where they got it?"

Eisenbarger looked away, squinting, toward Leaping Panther Mountain. "I don't know. Don't let it scare you. If you were going to get it from swimming with them, you'd probably have it by now."

Kevin giggled. "I'm not scared," he said. "I was getting scared, I think, when we were driving out here, but I'm *not* scared." He felt tears welling into his eyes and turned his head away from Eisenbarger and brushed at them. "I'm just sad," he said. "I'm so goddamn sad. We used to have such a time here. Jasper's one helluva guy, you know. He's just one *helluva* guy."

"Yes, I know," Eisenbarger said quietly.

"He'll never come here again. I won't either."

"No."

"Last time we were here, we were talking about going to college. You know what we decided?"

"What?"

"That we were going to El Paso and get laid."

Eisenbarger smiled.

"Will Jasper ever get laid again, do you think?"

"I don't know."

"That's important, you know, fucking."

"Yes."

92

"Some people pretend it isn't, but it is, isn't it?"

"Yes."

"Is there anything more important than that, Mr. Jay?"

The question rang an alarm in Eisenbarger's mind. He mentally flipped through every counseling book he had studied, then threw them away. The boy was looking for an honest answer. "Probably not," he said. "Not right now, anyway. Something might become more important later."

"What?"

"I don't know. It'll depend on what life deals out to you. Like Jasper. Getting laid probably isn't very important to him right now."

Kevin stared into the dead tank for a long time. Then he said, "I can't figure it out. Why was *he* the one? Why is *Jasper* the first case of polio Fort Appleby ever had?"

"That's one of the questions of the ages, Kevin. Men always ask it when something terrible happens to them, or to someone they love."

"Do they ever get any answers?"

"They get lots of answers. None of them is very satisfying, though."

"What's the best one?"

"Well, the most honest answer is another question. Why *not* Jasper?"

"Shit."

"Yeah. Let's go."

They climbed down the ladder and walked back across the pasture, detouring occasionally to avoid a prickly pear. When Eisenbarger slammed the pickup door, he turned to Kevin. "Kevin," he said, "be careful."

A fly was buzzing in Kevin's room when he went to bed. Kevin heard it, and wondered how it had escaped the DDT. It continued its sporadic whirr after Kevin turned out the light, and kept him from falling asleep right away. He dreamed that it was huge, and that its head was a human skull, covered with flaking gray algae.

Seven

Eisenbarger watched Kyle Kimbrow unpack his bulky wire recorder, unwind and plug in cords, and place the microphone on his desk. "Do you have to do this for *all* your interviews?"

"Yeah. KQLB doesn't have the greatest equipment in the business."

Eisenbarger was disappointed that Kimbrow in person was just as he had imagined him from his voice. He was tall and heavy, redheaded, with one of those flat-top haircuts with long hair on the sides, combed back over his ears, and a curl in front, trained to drip down his low, furrowed forehead. He wore the kind of cowboy clothing that only town people wear. A pearl-snapped gray shirt, too tight around a sagging torso, with dark sweat marks in the armpits; a Sears Roebuck western belt, gray whipcord trousers, also too tight, and intricately stitched blue boots with crepe soles and walking heels. Although Eisenbarger's office fan was on, large beads of sweat covered Kimbrow's freckled forehead and nose.

"There," Kimbrow said. "I think we're ready now."

"Good."

"Mind if I turn off this fan? It'll mess up the recording if we leave it on."

"Turn it off, then. Do whatever you have to."

"That's why I asked you to meet me here. I figured it would be quieter than at your house. All kinds of noises

94

interfere. If it's okay with you, I'll do a lead-in before I start asking you questions."

"Fine."

Kimbrow pulled a crumpled sheet of white paper from his hip pocket and unfolded it. He grinned at Eisenbarger. "Okay, here we go." He cleared his throat and flipped a switch on the recorder. He read into the microphone. His voice was nasal, high pitched.

"This is Kyle Kimbrow, reporting from Fort Appleby High School. Not many days ago, these halls and classrooms were teeming with the talk and laughter of the children of this small mountain town, who were returning to the halls of learning after a summer of fun and frolic. But today, all is silence. Fort Appleby, which never before experienced a case of infantile paralysis, has suddenly been stricken with four cases. No one knows how long the angel of disease will linger, and local school officials, fearing the worst, have shut down the school. With me here is Mr. John J. Eisenbarger, the school's principal. He's the only inhabitant of the building today. Mr. Eisenbarger, is Fort Appleby having a polio epidemic?"

"Yes. But before we go any further, I want to correct something you just said. The school board did *not* close the schools because we fear the worst. For all we know, the worst may already be over. We closed the schools as a simple safety precaution. We thought the children might be safer at home, scattered out, than sitting together under one roof. That's all."

"How bad an epidemic is it, Mr. Eisenbarger?"

"It depends on how you look at it, Mr. Kimbrow. Fort Appleby's history goes back nearly a hundred years, and during that time it has experienced only four cases of polio. That's a better record than nearly any other town in Texas.

On the other hand, four cases at *one time*, in a town of eight hundred people, is a pretty serious epidemic, statistically, at least."

"Are many people leaving town to escape the disease?"

"I haven't heard of *anyone* leaving. Have you? Many people from *other* places, particularly large cities, come *here* to escape the disease. Where would Fort Appleby people go? Houston? Dallas? San Antonio? El Paso?"

"Are you saying that people are safer here than in other towns?"

"I don't know. We're probably at least as safe."

"Has the community taken any measures to combat the disease, other than closing the schools?"

"Well, it's difficult to combat something when you don't know its cause. Children and parents have been instructed to observe the usual precautions. Avoid swimming, avoid crowds, and so forth. The town was fogged with DDT two days ago, which should just about wipe out the flies, if *they* have anything to do with polio. Water samples have been taken from all the wells, to be analyzed in Austin. If these things don't help, at least they've done no harm. Do *you* have any suggestions for us, Mr. Kimbrow?"

"Unfortunately, I don't, Mr. Eisenbarger. Tell me, who was the *first* polio victim in Fort Appleby?"

"Jasper Birdsong, one of our seniors."

"Is it fair to say that Jasper has been one of the best six-man football players in the state?"

"I would say that's fair, yes."

"Will Jasper ever play football again?"

"Not for Fort Appleby High. He'll be in the hospital for some time, and he's a senior this year."

"Will he ever play for somebody *else*? In college, I mean."

"How should *I* know, Mr. Kimbrow? Jasper's very talented, but very few good six-man players make college teams. They're usually not heavy enough."

"What I mean is, will Jasper be physically *able* to play football again?"

"I have no way of knowing that, Mr. Kimbrow. I suggest you ask his doctor."

"Fort Appleby has been district champion two years in a row. That's an enviable record."

"Yes."

"Is it true that the entire football season has been canceled this year, because of the epidemic?"

"Well, Fort Henderson forfeited to us last week. I understand that Castalon may forfeit this week. We're taking it one week at a time."

"If Castalon shows up Friday, will Fort Appleby have a team on the field to meet them?"

"Ask Coach Wilson about that. He knows a lot more about the football team than I do."

"Well, thank you, Mr. Eisenbarger, and good luck. I'm sure all the folks out there in the KQLB listening area will be praying for you and Jasper and Fort Appleby."

"That might be helpful."

"This is Kyle Kimbrow, KQLB News, reporting from besieged Fort Appleby High School."

Kimbrow shut off the recorder and flipped the switch to rewind the wire. Eisenbarger leaned back in his chair. "Would you turn the fan back on, Mr. Kimbrow?"

"Sure. You want me to play back the interview for you?"

"No, thanks. Do you consider it a *good* interview?"

"Yeah. I was hoping it would be more dramatic, though."

"Well, why didn't you ask me about the *other* polio victims? There are four of them, you know. In fact, the grandfather of one of them is working right down the hall. Why don't you interview him?"

"Who's that?"

"His name is Eduardo Rodriguez. Juanito Rodriguez is his grandson."

"Oh, yeah. The Meskin kid."

"Yes. Ask *him* a few questions. It might be pretty dramatic."

"Yeah? Well, I thought I'd just spotlight Jasper Birdsong. He's something of a public figure, you know. Names make the news, and all that."

"Juanito Rodriguez is a name, isn't he?"

Kimbrow didn't reply. He busied himself with the recorder, unplugging and winding up cords, fitting the lid back into its hinges. Eisenbarger watched him, rocking gently in his chair. "Speaking of the dramatic, Mr. Kimbrow, do you know Mrs. Smith?"

Kimbrow looked up. "Smith? Here in Fort Appleby?"

"No. The Mrs. Smith who makes the bread."

Kimbrow's brow wrinkled quizzically. "No. Is there such a person?"

"Coach, would you tell our radio audience what kind of boy Jasper Birdsong is?"

"I'd be glad to, Kyle. Jasper is as fine a boy and as fine an athlete as you'd want to meet. He's a clean-living, Christian young man. He made All-District last year, you know."

"Would you consider him good material for a college team?"

"I sure would. I think any college would be glad to have him. Would have, anyway."

"This is a terrible thing that's happened to him, isn't it?"

"It sure is. Terrible. Tragic, I would say."

"Well, Coach, how do things look otherwise?"

"Fine, Kyle. We have a young man named Clay Sanger that we've been grooming for Jasper's place. Jasper's a senior this year, you know. Clay's a sophomore, still a little green. But he's coming along. When we get back on the field again, folks are going to notice him. And then we've got Kevin Adams and Julio Garcia. They made All-District last year, too. We've won District two years in a row, you know."

"But what about your schedule? Hasn't it been canceled?"

"Oh, no! This polio thing isn't going to last much longer. When it's over, we'll be back on the field with all the rest. We'll be the champions again."

"What about the future, Coach? What about next year?"

"Well, we're losing four good boys out of our starting lineup this year, but we've got more coming up. I think we'll be right back there in contention again next year."

"I'm glad to catch you in such good spirits, Coach. Especially after this tragedy that you've suffered."

"Well, Kyle, you've got to roll with the punches. We've had a lot of blessings, too."

Eight

When they brought Juanito Rodriguez back to Fort Appleby, Eduardo's house was filled with weeping. Ernestina lay on the daybed, trying to sleep. But her slender body would shudder, and she would wake up weeping. Eduardo helped her up the stairs, took off her skirt and blouse, and turned back the covers on the big rosewood fourposter where Rafael Rodriguez had died under the big buffalo robe, clutching his Henry rifle. Ernestina was heavy against him as he eased her onto the feather mattress. He pulled the sheet and the crocheted counterpane up to her chin. "Sleep," he said.

He spent the morning beside Dolores, who sat in her rocker near the casket, her shoulders hunched under a heavy black shawl, as if she felt a chill. She had rocked all morning, without stopping. From time to time, she would moan, and mutter something. Eduardo never caught her words, but he would pat her shoulder. He wished the rocker didn't squeak every time she rocked. He must repair it, one of these days.

Gilberto, dry-eyed, handsome in his black suit and white shirt, greeted the weeping visitors at the door. They all embraced him and kissed him, and he spoke to them in a low voice. They would walk to the casket, look in and cross themselves, then squeeze Dolores's hand, and shake Eduardo's, and leave. Some knelt and said the Rosary. Some brought dishes of food, wrapped in white towels or wax paper, and left them on the kitchen cabinet.

Eduardo wished the funeral-home people hadn't placed the casket in front of the fireplace. Juanito's bassinet had stood there, and when Eduardo moved his eyes to the casket, he always, for just a second, saw the bassinet. He wanted to move the casket and its green-velvet-curtained cart to the other side of the room, but he thought it might not be proper. Also, he couldn't do it without seeing Juanito in there, and he didn't want to see him again. The funeral-home people hadn't known him before he was dead, and had made him too pale and too quiet. They had made him look like an angel, and Juanito, even when he slept, always looked sly and boisterous and brown.

In the early afternoon, when the sun began creeping across the daybed in the corner, Eduardo walked across the room, averting his eyes when he passed the casket, and pulled down the windowshades. He whispered into Gilberto's ear. Gilberto nodded, and Eduardo patted his shoulder and walked through the dark house and out the back door.

The wooden gate closed with a loud *swak*. Eduardo blinked several times to adjust his eyes to the glare of the dusty road and the gravel schoolyard on the other side. When he reached the door, he fumbled in his pocket for his keys, found the one that fit the lock, and was irritated at how long it took his hand to work it into the hole. He swung the door open and breathed deeply. The familiar odors of fuel oil, paint, floorwax, and chalk relaxed him, comforted him.

He switched on the light in the windowless room and sat down in the tattered green easy chair in the corner opposite the huge furnace. On the small table beside him were his electric coffeepot and tin cup and a stack of several years' issues of *Popular Mechanics*. Gilberto and Ernestina had given him the subscription for Christmas years ago, and had renewed it ever since. He enjoyed the magazine. He reached for the copy on top of the stack now, but changed his mind and let his hand drop into his lap. He gazed around the room, neither his eyes nor his mind really focusing on the paint buckets, pushbrooms, dustpans, hoses, wrenches, screwdrivers, or variously colored, firmly sealed cans that surrounded him. Then he saw his overalls and khaki work shirt hanging on the hook beside the work bench, and remembered. He got up, took off his blue suit-coat, folded it neatly, laid it across the back of his chair, and loosened his tie.

When he had changed clothes, he felt better. The over-alls and heavy work shoes fitted his body in an intimate, friendly way that his other clothes, especially the blue suit, never had. He transferred his pocketknife, keys, wallet, loose change, and watch from the suit to the overalls, picked up the burlap-covered water jug from the work bench, and filled it at the deep sink where he filled his mop buckets. He gathered up his shovel, crowbar, and pick from their corner by the door, lifted them to his shoulder, and carried them out to the black pickup that belonged to the school. He laid the tools in the back and the jug in the floorboard, then returned to slam the furnace-room door, turning the knob to make sure it was locked.

As he passed the post office, he noticed that the mail truck had arrived, and that several cars were parked there. The people in them were chatting, waiting for the postmaster to put their letters into their boxes. Eduardo was relieved that none of them noticed him. They didn't have to decide whether to smile when they waved at him, and he didn't have to decide whether he should wave in return, or merely nod. Friendly exchanges between grieving people and people who weren't grieving had always bothered Eduardo, and he avoided them whenever he could without seeming unfriendly. Grieving people were different from others, and it was a strain for the others to pretend that they either shared the grief or were unaware of it. Eduardo had wished before that God would make grieving people invisible until they recovered from the heavy shock of their loss. It would make death easier for everyone.

Eduardo passed Leaping Panther's paws and turned his eyes toward Old Fort Appleby, as he always did. He wished he could have seen it in his father's day, when people stood in front of the buildings and cheered whenever the Butterfield Stage rolled in with Rafael Rodriguez on the box. For some reason that he didn't understand, the stage, in his imagination, always arrived at night, with chimney smoke curling dimly into a clear, starry sky, and lamps in the officers' quarters and barracks casting soft, yellow shafts of light through the windows onto the dark parade ground.

Maybe that was the way his father had described it to him. He didn't remember.

He turned up Victorio Canyon and aimed the pickup up the narrow blacktop between Star Mountain on the left and the apple orchards along Victorio Creek on the right. A few pickers were at work in one of the orchards, climbing up tall stepladders and disappearing into the leaves, like angels in a Christmas pageant. Not far beyond the orchards, he had to shift into second, and his ears started popping. He opened his mouth to equalize the pressure. How long had it been since he had gone this high into the mountains? So long he had forgotten about the pressure.

Yet nothing had changed. The turnoff was just over the crest of the hill, and easy to miss, but Eduardo remembered and turned. Something *had* changed. There was a sign, in welded iron curlicues, painted silver, arching over the cattle-guard.

Ⓑ

CARL BIRDSONG

The cattle-guard pipes were loose, and their rattle when Eduardo drove across them stirred two buzzards from an old cottonwood by the creek. They pumped their long black wings laboriously upward until they knew that the iron rattle meant them no danger, then relaxed into a lazy soar, slowly circling back to their perch. Eduardo had always admired the buzzards, despite their hideous appearance. By hiding the stink of death in their entrails, they served a higher purpose than most birds.

The creek was a brackish trickle, barely enough to wet the treads of Eduardo's tires as he bounced across the water-rounded stones of its bed. He shifted into low to climb the bank, then leveled off onto the road Rafael and Dietrich had gouged into the slope of Knob Hill. The boulders strewn below him, he knew, had been shoved by their naked arms and shoulders to the spots where they would sit until the end of the world.

When Eduardo rounded the curve to the headquarters, Jimmy George Duncan was in the corral, shoeing his big roan gelding. The foreman peered between the fence rails when he heard the pickup, dropped the hoof, and was closing the gate when Eduardo stopped. Jimmy George walked awkwardly, squinting wearily at his visitor.

"*Hola!*" he said.

"*Hola.*"

"Eduardo, I'm sorry . . ."

"Yes. It's hard."

Jimmy George nodded. "We know that here."

They paused uncomfortably, gazing each at the other. The roan pawed the ground with his unshod hoof.

"I want to bury Juanito here."

"I don't think Carl would mind."

Eduardo drove behind the headquarters house and found the narrow trail that wound up the hill with the grove of oaks on its crest. The hill was steeper and rockier than he remembered, and the trail hadn't been maintained. Wide gashes had been eroded across it. Eduardo, as he eased the pickup across them, wondered if the hearse could make it, and if the funeral-home people would be willing to try. No matter. They could use the pickup. Or he and Gilberto could carry Juanito up, as Rafael had been carried.

It had been Eduardo's decision to bury Rafael on the ranch, beside his friend. His mother lay in San Ignacio Cemetery. He didn't know where Maria Hawthorne was buried. He was proud of the granite double tombstone he had erected over the graves.

RAFAEL RODRIGUEZ   DIETRICH HAWTHORNE
1915   1897

He would have included the birthdates, had he known
them. He had always thought it strange that his father
didn't know how old he was.

Eduardo lifted the jug and the tools from the pickup and
carried them to the grove. He debated briefly whether to
dig the grave beside Rafael's, or apart from it, under another tree. He decided to put the child beside his great-
grandfather, the spot he had always considered his own.

Eduardo lifted the heavy pick above his head and swung
it with all the strength he could gather. It barely penetrated
the brown, matted grass. The thin topsoil under the grass
had dried almost to stone in the summer's drought.
Eduardo paused in dismay, suddenly remembering that he
didn't know how long to make the grave. It would be terrible to carry Juanito all this way, and then find that he
wouldn't fit into the hole that his grandfather had dug for
him.

Eduardo decided to dig it six feet long. It was dark when
he finished. The evening breeze chilled his sweaty skin, and
his hands were bleeding.

Nine

Elmer Martin stood with George Wilson at the window,
watching the cars roll slowly by. He moved his hand over
his bald head as if combing invisible hair. "Gives you the
creeps, don't it?" he said.

Wilson shook his head. "It's a shame and a pity. Cute
little fellow, too."

"Yep. It gives you the creeps. I can't remember the last time a kid died in this town. I've lived here twenty-three years, and I can't remember another kid dying." Martin raised his cup and sucked at his coffee.

"Hey, look," Wilson said. "There's Jay."

"Yep. By himself. Must be representing the school."

"Shit. I should have gone with him. But funerals give me the creeps. Especially Catholic funerals. All that mumbo-jumbo."

"Well, one representative of the school is enough. I bet old Eduardo won't even notice that he's there, anyway. I guess he's pretty tore up."

"Can't blame him."

"Nope. Can't blame him. Tough, losing your only grand-kid."

The screen door slammed. Willie Joe Callahan, in his deputy garb, slapped Wilson on the rump. "Hi, Coach. Hey, Elmer, you're the only one that didn't close up for the funeral."

"Should have, I guess. I didn't figure everybody in town was going to it, though. Why ain't you directing traffic?"

"All the traffic's going to the funeral. They don't need me to show them the way. How about a cup of coffee?"

Wilson raised his empty cup. "I'll buy."

They moved to the soda fountain. Wilson and Callahan slid onto stools, and Martin went behind the fountain, refilled Wilson's cup and his own, and pulled a clean one down from the shelf for Callahan. He waved away Wilson's dime. "Keep your money. It's on me."

Callahan touched Wilson's shoulder with his crippled hand. "Well, Coach, who we beating this week?"

"Geneva."

"Geneva! They ain't lost a game yet. Think you can take them?"

106

"It isn't funny, Willie Joe."

"Sorry."

"That son of a bitch Dick Hamilton called me last night, begging me to forfeit. I gave him some language you wouldn't want to hear repeated, preacher."

"Is *he* going to forfeit?"

"He *says* he isn't. He *says* he's going to show up and see if we put a team out there to play him."

"He's bluffing," Martin said.

"Sure he is." Wilson waved toward the street. "After this, what mama's going to let her son come here? Kimbrow's had this kid's death on the news for three days now."

Martin moved around the counter and slid onto the stool beside Wilson. The three drank in silence, staring gloomily at their images in the backbar mirror.

"Well, I guess this ruins any chance of school starting again soon," Callahan said. "Ada Lou's going nuts, with six kids underfoot all the time. The kids are going nuts, too. Bored out of their minds."

"Hell, *everybody's* going nuts!" Wilson said. "How can we help it? I think we ought to start school again and get things back to normal."

"But George!" Martin said. "A kid just died, for Chrissake! I'm a member of the school board. You think I'm going to take the responsibility . . ."

"No, Elmer. You're right. I know that. But we can't do *anything* right. A kid died, right? He's got to have a funeral, right? Half the town's at the funeral, right? What's one of the things we're supposed to avoid? Crowds! Now half the people at that funeral are going to wake up tonight thinking *they've* got polio. Maybe in a week or two we'll find out one or two of them were *right*. Shit, man, we can't do *anything* right!"

"You think the kid shouldn't have a funeral?" Callahan said.

"Oh, hell, preacher! I'm just saying it shouldn't be a *public* funeral. The family and the priest should go out there and lay him in the ground real nice and quiet, and the rest of us should send sympathy cards. But half the town is driving out to the Circle-B, where we've had two cases of polio . . . Why are they burying him out there, anyway?"

"The Rodriguezes have some kind of family graveyard out there," Martin said. "They used to live out there, years ago."

"Well, I just think we ought to start school again and get things back to normal," Wilson said. "It would be better than just sitting around looking at each other and traipsing off to funerals."

"If school started tomorrow, I bet nobody would show up," Martin said.

Wilson shrugged. "Whatever we do, it's going to be wrong."

"Dear Emmy,

"It's funny, I've known you all my life, and have never written you a letter before. Of course, we've always lived right here in Fort Appleby (groan) so it would have been kind of silly, I guess. Anyway, I've been thinking about you a lot and thought you might like to hear from your beautiful (Ha!) niece and find out what's going on in the Big City. Believe me, it's a lot."

Rosa Hawthorne reclined on her bed against her green-and-gold Fort Appleby Warriors pillow. She still wore the black dress she had worn to Juanito's funeral, but she had taken off her shoes and hose and garter belt. They lay in a small heap at the foot of the bed, between the ragged toy dog that she had kept from her childhood and the large,

108

fluffy panda that Julio Garcia had won for her last year when a carnival visited Fort Appleby. Rosa bit the end of her fountain pen, wondering whether Emmy knew about Juanito. She decided that she didn't want to be the one to tell him.

"I went over to Cora Aguilar's house yesterday to help her bleach her hair. She decided she wanted to be a sexy blonde like Marilyn Monroe. But we worked and worked, and it just came out kind of gray. Cora cried, and we ruined four of Mrs. Aguilar's towels. I think Cora hates me now, but that's all right, because I never liked her much anyway, ever since that time when we caught that burro in the street and decided to have the rodeo in our backyard. You remember that, Emmy? She got mad because we wouldn't let her ride, and turned the burro loose while we were in the house begging Mama for Kool-Aid. She always was a shit, and I don't think it's bad to be hated by a shit, do you?"

The memory of nine-year-old Emmy astride the drowsy burro, whacking the beast with a yucca pole, trying to make him buck, brought a tightness to Rosa's throat. She saw his red hair blazing in the sun, the puffs of dust rising from the burro's gray hide under Emmy's pole. She saw Cora at the fence, glaring between the wires, sucking her thumb. So long. So long ago. She would write no more of that.

"Well, let me see what else has happened. Oh yes! The Calderons bought a brand new Chevy last week. It's green, and Sonny drives it all over town with his elbow sticking out of the window, thinking all the girls are going to whistle at him. He says Willie Joe Callahan stopped him for speeding the other night and chewed him out, and that he gave Willie Joe the finger. Do you believe that? I don't. I think if Willie Joe ever stopped Sonny, Sonny would pee in his pants and cry."

Yes, this was the kind of letter Emmy would like. It would

make him smile. Could Emmy smile? She wouldn't think about that, either.

"They killed a lobo out on the Lucky 7 the other day, and one of their wetbacks put it in the back of his pickup and brought it to town. He parked in front of the drugstore, and everybody went around and looked at it. It was like the circus had come to town or something. People are *so* silly! It *was* a big lobo, though. The wetback said he was over three feet high, standing up. He had great big teeth, and his tongue was hanging out. I didn't know lobos looked so much like dogs. I felt sorry for him. They say he must have come up from Mexico. Why would he do that?"

Emmy would answer that question someday. He would remember it long after she had forgotten she had asked it, and tell her all about lobos. One time, he told her about how rattlesnakes lose their skins every year, and she didn't believe him, even after he found an abandoned snake skin and showed it to her. She believed he somehow had taken it off of a dead snake. It was years later, in the sixth grade, that her teacher told her Emmy was right. By then, he had forgotten that she didn't believe him, so she didn't tell him he was right.

"I tell you, Emmy, I don't know what gets into people sometimes. You know what's a big thing around here now? Yo-yos! Elmer Martin got a box of them and put them in the candy case at the drugstore, and everybody bought them like crazy. Now every store in town is selling them, even the cafe. The boys paint fancy flowers and hearts on them and give them to their girlfriends, like class rings or something. Alfonso Lopez and Benny Williams were doing tricks with yo-yos in front of the drugstore the other day, and their strings got all tangled up together, and they got into a fight. Well, they didn't really fight. They circled around a lot and cussed at each other. Then Benny's little brother untangled the strings and they stood around look-ing silly. The girls haven't figured out what to do with the yo-yos when the boys give them to them, but everybody is just *dying* to have one. No, I don't have one (groan!)."

Tears dropped to the paper, smearing the ink.

"Oh, Emmy, it's all a lie!," she wrote. "The yo-yo thing happened years ago, and you know it. Juanito is dead, and you're dying, and I'm in love with Kevin Adams, and he hates me! Fucking *gringo!* Life is shitty, Emmy! *Shitty!*"

She tore the paper into tiny pieces and flung it at the stuffed animals. The pieces floated back to the bed like snow. She grabbed a Kleenex from the box on the bedside table and wiped her eyes and blew her nose. Then she took another piece of writing paper from the box and started again.

"Dear Emmy,

I was at church today, and lots of candles were burning for you. We miss you.

"Love,
"Rosa

"P.S. How do you like my new writing paper? It has perfume on it. Hold it to your nose, and it'll make you *extremely passionate!!*"

Ten

What's happening to our children? What's happening to our children? Willie Joe Callahan couldn't get the question out of his head. The harder he tried to shut it away, the louder it echoed. Answers popped like Roman candles. Abraham and Isaac. He couldn't forget the astonishment on all those faces when he offered them that. A jealous god.

Sin. The fathers have eaten sour grapes, and the children's teeth are set on edge. Not chance. Not blind chance. There's a plan. Suffering. Suffering wins things. Job. Jesus. Isn't that what it's all about? Place your hand in the nail-scarred hand? His yoke is easy and his burden is light? Not a sparrow falls from the air . . .

He squinted past the sweep of the windshield wipers. The raindrops shot across the headlight beams like pellets of crystal. In Fort Appleby, the drumming of rain would awaken people, urging them to front porches to stand in pajamas and bathrobes to watch. Some would dress and drive to the ranches. He would tell Carl Birdsong . . . What's happening to our children?

He glanced into the rearview mirror. He could see nothing. "How's she doing, Ada Lou?"

"She's sleeping."

The small hairs rose on his neck. It's what the Perkins woman had said. She's sleeping.

"Maybe we should have taken her to Sharon," Ada Lou said. "Maybe Dr. Roberts . . ."

"No. We'll find out faster this way."

Anna Kathleen was his oldest, his favorite. Fifteen. Smart. Prettier than the others.

"It's a long way," Ada Lou said.

"We're almost there." He pointed ahead at the black desert night. The lights of Abilene, still beyond the horizon, were reflected eerily by the invisible, rain-swollen clouds.

Then there were streetlights along the highway. He reached to turn on the siren and the flashing red light. Tears blurred his vision. The big Ford jumped the center island. It overturned, rolled across the other lanes in a hell of bending, grinding, tearing metal, and came to rest, upside down, against a utility pole.

Callahan saw the cracks spread across the windshield like a magic spiderweb, but he heard none of it. Hands grabbed him, dragged him. The flashing pink neon sign said Kerry's Kustard Kastle. The man was fat. He wore a long white apron and a white paper cap.

"You okay, buddy?"

Callahan nodded.

"It's a goddamn miracle. Jesus."

He rode in the front seat beside the policeman. They were moving fast, the siren screaming. They told him to sit down on a bench in the corridor. The lights were very bright. "We'll be right with you," they said. They wheeled the two shiny carts with the snowy sheets past him, through the door at the end of the bench. They didn't close the door.

"Dead," they said.

"So's this one," they said.

"Both of them. DOA."

The lights hurt his eyes. He got up and walked down the corridor. The ambulance was still backed up to the door. He stepped around it, into the rain. He walked down the narrow driveway and turned into the parking lot. The rain was like crystal pellets in the beams of the lights. The car tops were like smooth glass.

He dragged the revolver from its holster. The weight of it dragged his hand down.

"Don't do it, preacher. Not yet, anyway."

He turned. The blonde woman's hair was wet and stringy. She was hugging herself, shivering. She held out her hand.

"Give it to me," she said.

He didn't move. She reached and gently pried his fingers from around the revolver.

"Come on, preacher. Walk with me."

She took his arm, and they walked slowly back toward the emergency entrance. They stepped back into the brightly lit corridor. Blood was seeping out of his boot.

"See, you're hurt," she said.

OCTOBER, 1952

One

Mary Beth didn't hear him walk in. She looked up, and he was standing on the other side of the kitchen table, turning back the cuffs of his clean white shirt. He was wearing his gray whipcord dress-up trousers. His flat-top was waxed and brushed erect, his face shaven and shiny.

"You look nice. Going to church?"

"No. Abilene."

"Abilene!"

He walked around the table and kissed her lightly on the lips. "I have to visit a sick friend."

Mary Beth frowned. "Who's going with you?"

"Nobody."

"Abilene's a long way. I don't like it." She glanced down. "You shined your boots."

"Yes."

"They look nice. I'll go with you."

"No."

"You'll need somebody to talk to."

"I don't want to talk."

She gazed into her son's face. Just like his father. She stood up and hugged him. "Do you think Jasper wants to see you?"

"I hope so."

"Take my car. I don't want you on the highway in that crazy old Ford. I guess you'll need some money, too."

They walked to the living room together. Mary Beth rummaged in her big purse and handed him two bills. "Fifteen dollars is enough, isn't it?"

"Fine." He pecked her on the cheek.

"When will you be back?"

"Tonight. I just need to see Jasper."

"See Emmy and Brother Callahan, too, if you get a chance. They would appreciate it."

She followed him to the front gate, clutching her robe to her, and waved when he turned the car into the street and headed it toward the plaza.

The fuel gauge pointed to full. The street was deserted. The drugstore, the grocery, the Leaping Panther Cafe, all were closed. So was the Gulf station.

The highway was narrow and hugged the snaky twists of Victorio Creek, but Kevin could have driven it blindfolded. He loved the canyon. It had been a favorite ambush site of the Apaches, and Kevin knew two spots along the roadside where settlers and stagecoach passengers had been murdered. At one of them, the remains of a crude stone barricade, which five desperate families had thrown together a few hours before they died, were still visible. Kevin pictured in his mind what the place must have looked like to the soldiers who came with wagons to pick up the mutilated men, the naked women and butchered children. He felt little sympathy for the victims. The mountains had belonged to the Indians, and he didn't blame them for trying to keep them. He had heard of the beauty of the hills in those days, before the cattle and the sheep, when the mountainsides weren't laced with barbed wire and the grass in the flats was as high as a man's stirrups. The old ones had heard it from their grandfathers and fathers and passed on their tales to the children, as Adam must have described Eden to Cain and Abel. Much of the beauty remained, despite even the drought. The short, tawny grass glistened in the morning sunlight on the slopes across the creek. Cloud shadows moved like silent animals, swiftly stalking, relentless and inescapable, even across the steep, dark brown palisades. Kevin was glad to be alone. He found himself humming "Warriors, Fight," and wondered whether he intended the song for himself or for those squat, bowlegged savages who had swooped down on the unfortunate travelers.

Thirty miles out of Fort Appleby, he topped Chief Nicholas Pass. Below him stretched the vast Buffalo Flat. It, too, was beautiful from the pass, pale blue, like a clean, placid lake. But he knew it would turn ugly as he wound his way down from the mountains. Cotton stalks would stand rotting in the fields. Near the gins, the roadsides, fences and utility lines would be covered with lint. Tiny drifts of sand would stand against the curbs in the tacky, makeshift towns. The men on the sidewalks would be wearing blue overalls and cracked, shapeless shoes, and grotesque farm machines would stand in lots with strings of pennants fluttering over them. Kevin hated the flat and its towns. He knew why cowmen and cowboys had killed farmers in the old days, and disliked them even now. He knew he would drive fast across the flat, glancing into the rearview mirror for the Highway Patrol, driving hard toward the desert to the east, and its endless spaces, untouched even by God, and its endless sky.

Beyond Odessa and the oil-field settlements, Kevin hit a long, straight stretch of highway without another car in sight. He glanced into the mirror. The highway behind him was empty, too. He breathed a long sigh, and smiled. He had never felt so alone and so free. Suddenly he pulled onto the shoulder and hit the brake. His rear wheels skidded on the white gravel. He cut the ignition, got out, and stood very still beside the car. The only sound was the ticking of the engine cooling. He needed to get away from even that. He walked down the short slope into the borrow-ditch, watching the fine white dust spoil his shine, then crawled through the barbed-wire fence and into the desert, making his way carefully through the creosote bushes and the cacti, trying to avoid kicking the sharp white stones. Fifty yards from the highway, he stopped beside a huge and very old mesquite. Its lacy leaves were moving slowly, silently, although Kevin could feel no breeze. He wondered if plants breathe, if the tree was panting in the hot noon. In the distance, a single locust whirred the only sound in the flat, chalky land and dark green, waist-high forest. He wondered if the desert was ever really silent, or if even death was silent. Even in the grave, perhaps, there was a locust or a god whirring softly in the distance, whispering to the silent generations of ancestors and descendants, of angels and devils and things to come.

Kevin turned full-circle. As far as he could see, on the land and in the sky, his was the only animal life. He felt small in the immensity of his surroundings, great in his superiority to all about him, as if he were either the first man or the last man on earth. "I am Kevin Adams!" he shouted. But the sound seemed to die, to be absorbed into the vast silence, only inches from his lips. He wondered why he hadn't read of this, why some poet or novelist hadn't come here, and stood here, and written about being a creature in the desert. He would ask Eisenbarger if someone had.

Despite the heat of the day, he suddenly yearned for a fire. He took a step toward a dead creosote bush, intending to gather twigs and sit for an hour or two beside the mesquite, feeding the flame. Then he heard the whine of a semi's tires. He heard the sharp *whoosh* when the driver hit the air brakes. He loped toward the fence. The driver opened his door and stepped onto the running board.

"You okay?" he called.

"Yeah. Just taking a leak."

"Thought you might be having some car trouble."

"No. Thanks for stopping, though."

"Okay. Take it easy."

"Right. You, too."

The driver slammed the door, waved, and began easing the semi through its many gears. The truck was still in sight, roaring, belching, whining, when Kevin reached the barbed wire and crawled through.

Later, he stopped at a Texaco station and drank a Coke and ate a bag of Tom's Toasted Peanuts while the man filled the tank. "You know where Hendricks Memorial Hospital is?" he asked.

"Yeah. Just a minute. I'll draw you a map." The man stooped and peered at the gas-tank hole. "You got a relative there?"

"A friend."

"Not polio, I hope."

"Yes. Polio."

"Tough shit. It's really been racking them up this year. Where you from?"

"A little town up in the mountains. Fort Appleby."

"I know where it's at. Took my vacation out there once. God's country. Didn't know they had polio out there."

"We didn't, until this year. Four cases so far."

"Shit. Don't seem that no place is safe no more, what with the war and the Russians and the A-bomb, and Commies crawling all over Washington, and this polio shit."

"Yeah, you're right."

The man straightened, replaced the gas-tank cap, and shut down the pump. "Come inside. I'll draw you that map."

He drew a good map. Despite his unfamiliarity with the city, Kevin found the hospital without difficulty. Its vastness surprised him. He had never been in such a huge building. In the lobby, a gray-haired woman gave him directions to the polio ward. The large glass doors were directly across the corridor from the elevator. Kevin peered through the glass at the two long rows of shiny iron lungs arranged along the walls of the large room. It looked like a warehouse, except for the starched nurses and orderlies moving slowly along the aisle from one stainless-steel cylinder to another, and the motionless heads protruding from the cylinders, resting on gleaming white pillows. The machines breathed softly, in long, slow breaths, like huge animals sleeping. Kevin felt as if he were watching a science-fiction movie, or standing in the middle of a brightly lighted nightmare. His breath had quickened. As he extended his hand to the door-handle, he almost expected it to recede, or disappear, and he would awaken, sweating and trembling, but relieved that he had only been dreaming.

"Kevin!"

He turned toward the voice. Carl Birdsong was hurrying along the corridor, his old-fashioned high bootheels thudding on the tile. He was older than Kevin remembered him, his gray hair thinner and longer, his weathered face more deeply wrinkled, almost as gray as his hair.

"Lordy, boy! Who would have thought it!"

"Hello, Mr. Birdsong."

"It's great of you to come. Jasper's not in there. He's got a private room." Birdsong grabbed Kevin's elbow and steered him down the long corridor. His dark brown eyes were bright now, smiling. "I'm so glad you're here." Then his voice dropped. "Listen, son, when we go in there, try not to act surprised. It would make him feel . . . Try not to act shocked, okay?"

The words frightened Kevin. He wanted to pull away from Birdsong's grasp. He nodded.

Birdsong quietly swung open the door. The venetian blind was pulled shut over the room's single window. A long, pitifully skinny form, wearing only white jockey shorts, lay in cave-like gloom on ghostly sheets. The eyes were closed. "Jesus!" Kevin whispered. The long black hair was fanned out on the pillow. The face beneath it was a mere skull with large ears, sharp nose and cheekbones, and pale skin drawn tightly over it. The once-muscular, dark body had shrunk to a real-life replica of the plaster emaciated Jesus above the altar of San Ignacio Church. The iron lung, glowing softly beside the bed, caught Kevin's eye. It was smaller than he had imagined them. "Does he know about the others?" he whispered.

"Only Emmy. He saw Gregorio pass the door one day. Gregorio visits him now. Go on in, son."

"Mr. Birdsong, I can't stay long."

"They had to cut a hole in his throat when we came, so he could breathe. He shouldn't try to talk. He's been wanting to see you, though." Birdsong leaned over the bed and spoke into Jasper's ear. "Hey, son. Look who's here." Jasper's eyes fluttered open. Birdsong adjusted the blind to let in the sunlight. The brown eyes grew large with recognition.

"Hi, Jasper." Kevin almost asked Jasper how he was feeling, then caught himself and just stood at the foot of the bed, grinning.

Jasper's lips moved, and a deep, rough growl emerged from the thin chest.

Birdsong leaned close. "What?"

The growl came again.

"He wants to know how you are," Birdsong said.

"Oh, I'm fine. Alicia's fine . . ." He wished he hadn't mentioned Alicia. Her name made him wonder if Jasper would ever fuck again. He didn't want Jasper to think about

123

that. "Everybody's thinking about you, buddy, wondering how you're getting along."

"We've gotten a lot of get-well cards," Birdsong said. "We just haven't gotten around to . . . I guess I ought to write a note to Elmer Martin and tell him to tack it up in the drugstore or something."

The growl came again. Birdsong bent close, then raised his head. "He wants to know about school," he said.

"Well . . ." Kevin hesitated, looking to Birdsong for guidance. Birdsong nodded. "They closed the school, buddy, after you and Emmy got sick. We haven't gone back. They don't want to take any chances, I guess . . ." Kevin was afraid he had gone too far. "Well, I guess that's about it. Fort Appleby's as dull as it always was. You'll still recognize it when you get back."

The dark eyes turned soft and dreamy. Their gaze moved from Kevin to Birdsong, who bent and listened to the growl.

"Jasper wants you to keep his car for him. He's probably afraid that old jalopy will die if it doesn't get any exercise . . ." Birdsong flushed and plunged his fists deep into his pockets.

"I've got your car," Kevin said. "I'll take good care of it. It'll be in good shape when you get home." He could find nothing more to say, but he remained at the foot of the bed, where the brown eyes could see him.

"Sit down, son," Birdsong said, moving a blanket off of the only chair.

"No, thanks. I'd better shove off. How's Mrs. Birdsong?"

"Fine. She's at the motel sleeping now. We take turns."

"Well, it's nice seeing you, Jasper. Get well and hurry back, hear?"

Birdsong walked out to the corridor with Kevin. "That'll help a lot," he said. "We appreciate it."

124

"Where's Emmy? I ought to say hello. Carmelita will ask."

Birdsong pointed. "Six doors down the hall, on this side. I'll come with you."

"That's okay. I can find it."

The door to Emmy's room was open, but Gregorio was asleep in the chair. Kevin heard the iron lung breathing. He didn't go in.

He was the only customer in the Four Leaf Clover Truck Stop when the waitress refilled his coffee cup. "Where you from?" she asked.

He glanced up. She was a short, baby-faced blonde. She wore a class ring on a thin golden chain around her neck. "Fort Appleby."

"You're Kevin Adams, ain't you?"

"Yes, I am. How did you know?"

She flashed him a coy smile and slid into the other side of the booth. She set the glass coffee pot on the table between them. "Surprised you, didn't I?"

"Sure did. How did you know?"

"I graduated at Castalon last year. I used to watch you play football. You're good."

"We beat you, didn't we?"

"Sure did." She giggled. "I used to wish you'd ask me for a date after the game."

"I didn't know you."

"I know. You look tired. Where you going?"

"Home."

"Where you been?"

"Abilene."

"What for?"

"Went to see a friend in the hospital. Jasper Birdsong. You remember him?"

"Sure do. What's the matter with him?"

"Polio."

"You're shitting me!"

"No."

"Jesus! Bad?"

"Real bad."

"Jesus H. Christ!"

She played with the ring on the chain and gazed at him appraisingly. "You alone, or are you picking up somebody somewhere?"

"I'm alone."

"Well, hey, I get off in an hour. Maybe we could go somewhere."

"Can't. I'm tired, and I've got a long drive ahead of me. And I feel like shit."

"I wasn't thinking of going far."

"Like where?"

"Like over there." She pointed through the plate-glass window at the flickering neon motel sign.

Kevin picked up his cup and drank, peering at her over the rim. She smiled and stuck the tip of her tongue out at him.

"How much? For the room, I mean."

"Nothing. I live there."

"Alone?"

"Yeah." She giggled. "You could use some rest. And I've got some beer."

Kevin shrugged and smiled. "Okay. I'll have to call home, though."

"The phone's by the cash register."

He dropped the nickel in and dialed the operator. The waitress remained in the booth, smiling and playing with the ring.

"What's your name?" he asked.

"Emily," she said.

Two

Only a night light was on. Gregorio was cramped from slumping in the chair. The doctor in his white jacket and the pale nurse beside him, hugging herself as if she were cold, looked like angels in the gloom.

"What is it?"

"Wake up," the doctor said, shaking his shoulder again. "Wake up, sir."

The nurse shuddered and clasped her arms even more tightly across her thin chest. Gregorio saw now that she was young.

"I'm awake," he said. "I'm okay."

It was very quiet. He wondered how long he had slept. He didn't hear Emiliano's machine breathing. "What time is it?"

"Almost three o'clock." The doctor squatted and peered into his face. "There's something I've got to tell you."

"What is it?"

"Mr. Hawthorne, are you really awake now? Do you understand what I'm saying?"

"Yes."

"Mr. Hawthorne, your son is dead."

"What did you say?"

"Your son, Mr. Hawthorne. Emiliano. He died a few minutes ago. I'm sorry."

"Emiliano?"

"Yes. I'm sorry. When the nurse came in to check him, she found that he had expired. Had died."

The doctor turned to the young nurse. Her teeth were chattering. "Your first?"

"Yes."

"Go get that other guy from Fort Appleby. Down the hall."

"Birdsong."

"Yes. They know each other."

The nurse fled. Gregorio slumped back in his chair. The doctor stood up.

"We weren't expecting it, Mr. Hawthorne. He seemed to be doing okay. His heart apparently just got tired and stopped beating. That happens sometimes." The doctor hated these explanations. People live, they get sick, they die. The doctor didn't know why any of it happens, and trying to give reasons made him feel dishonest. He was relieved when the gray-haired man in the maroon bathrobe rushed into the room.

"Mr. Birdsong?"

"Yes."

"I guess she told you."

"I'm so sorry."

"You know Mr. Hawthorne, I think?"

"Yes. He works for me."

"I thought you might be of some help to him."

"I'll do what I can . . ."

"The patient was a Catholic, I believe."

"Yes."

"Shall I have someone call a priest?"

"Yes."

"I'll leave him to you, then. If you need anything, just ring for the nurse."

The doctor and the nurse left, pulling the door closed behind them. Birdsong knelt on the floor and grabbed Gregorio under his arms. He pulled his limp body toward himself and laid the shaggy head on his shoulder.

"Gregorio . . ."

"Carlos," Gregorio whispered, "Emiliano is dead. My Emiliano is dead."

"Yes. I know."

"*Is* he dead, Carlos?"

"Yes. He's dead."

Gregorio broke away from Birdsong's grasp. He walked stiffly across the room to the iron lung and peered through the gloom at Emiliano's still, pale head. He brushed a strand of red hair from the boy's forehead. "Carlos! He's warm!"

"He hasn't been dead long."

"He *is* really dead, then?"

"Yes. He's gone."

A strange sound, half sob and half laugh, burst from Gregorio's throat. "He's so skinny," he said. "Felipe, when he died, looked so strong. Emiliano, I could carry him by myself, like a baby."

"Gregorio, let's go downstairs. It's not good to stay here."

"But we must come back."

"Yes. When the priest comes."

Birdsong was glad to step into the garish fluorescent light of the corridor. He put his arm around Gregorio's thin shoulders, half hugging him, half supporting him. He had known Gregorio all his life. Gregorio had taught him to ride and rope. He had never lived on his land when Gregorio wasn't there, too. Yet this was the first time Birdsong could remember touching the old man since those early days when they sat in the same saddle. He was surprised at the hardness of the thin muscles under the khaki shirt, muscles that jerked and trembled as Gregorio leaned against him. The elevator door opened as soon as Birdsong pushed the button. He led Gregorio in and guided him into a corner. A muscle under the old man's right eye was twitching.

"He was a good boy," Gregorio said. "He was making you a good hand."

"One of the best. A little longer, and he would have been better than you."

"He couldn't rope worth a shit."

"But he was learning. A little longer, and he would have been better than you."

"I am old . . ."

The elevator door slid open, and they stepped across the hall into the cafeteria. The room was empty, except for two nurses hunched wearily over a small table, saying nothing, and a Mexican woman behind the empty steam table.

"Grab a booth," Birdsong said. "I'll get some coffee."

He filled two cups at the stainless-steel urn, then remembered that he was dressed in pajamas and robe. He looked at the Mexican woman, embarrassed, and she smiled. "It's okay," she said.

Gregorio shook his head as Birdsong set the cups on the table. "I've lived too long," he said. "I've seen all my sons die."

"It's God's will," Birdsong said.

"Yes. God's will."

They sucked slowly at the steaming coffee, as they had thousands of times around campfires and kitchen tables and in stockyard cafes. Birdsong guessed that Gregorio had taught him how to drink coffee, too. Gregorio was staring absently past Birdsong's head. His cheek was twitching. Birdsong pulled a pack of cigarettes from his robe pocket and offered it to Gregorio. Gregorio shook his head. Birdsong lit one and waved out the match. "I want to do something for you," he said, squinting through the smoke.

130

"Something for me?"

"I want to buy Emmy's cemetery plot for him. In Mountainview Cemetery."

"Mountainview? No. San Ignacio."

"Mountainview is a nicer place."

"But my family . . ."

"They're scattered all over San Ignacio. Emmy couldn't be buried beside any of them. He'll be cared for at Mountainview."

"Emiliano is a Mexican."

"If I tell them to bury him at Mountainview, by God, they will bury him at Mountainview."

"No."

"I'll buy the marker, too. A nice one."

"Carlos. Why?"

"My daddy told me to love you."

"Your daddy didn't love me."

"Maybe that's why he told *me* to."

"I'm too tired, Carlos."

"I'll call Elmer Martin in the morning. He takes care of the Cemetery Association."

"I don't think Emiliano would like being buried away from his people, Carlos."

"Gregorio . . . If Jasper goes, I'll bury him beside Emmy."

Gregorio shrugged. "Okay, Carlos. You're the boss."

"You want me to call Carmelita now?"

"No. In the morning."

Birdsong swallowed the last of his coffee. "Let's go see if that priest is here," he said.

Sweat poured down Kevin's face. Cold sweat. The sweat of fear that he had read about. He had always doubted that the sweat of fear was really cold, but it was. He had polio.

He knew it. He couldn't move his legs. He felt nothing in his legs. It was as if they were gone, as if someone had stolen through the darkness and severed them very quickly and taken them away. He felt no pain. Was that good or bad? Maybe he was dead. No, he was sweating. He would try to move his arm. *Could* he move his arm? Yes. There. It was moving. His hand dropped onto his bare chest. His skin was clammy. Ah. There was a heartbeat. Faint. Or was it the pulse in his fingertips? Did it matter? Would the pulse continue after the heart stopped beating? No. Of course not. His heart *was* beating. He was *not* dead. But his legs . . . Could he speak? What if he tried and a growl came out?

"Emily!"

The pale, naked body stirred softly. Her back was to him.

"Emily! Help me!"

He lifted his arm slowly and let it drop onto her shoulder. She rolled onto her back. Her face turned toward him.

"Emily! Help me!"

She rose onto an elbow, awake now, alarmed. "Honey! What's the matter?"

"I've got it!" His voice was a frantic whisper. "I've got it!"

"Got what, darling?" She was trying to remain calm, but there was fear in her voice, too.

"The polio! I've got polio!"

"Oh, God!" Then her voice became cool, analytical. "How do you know, honey? How do you feel?"

"My legs! There's no feeling in them! I can't move them! I can't *feel* anything!"

"You've been dreaming about old Jasper, haven't you?"

"I *mean* it, Emily!"

She pinched him on the thigh. "Did you feel that?"

"No. Wait. Yes, I think I did. Do it again. Yes, I did. Just a little."

She smiled at him through the darkness. "Little Emily will take care of you." She crawled on all fours to the foot of the bed and began, slowly, gently, to massage each of his toes. "Do you feel that?"

"Yes. I think so. Yes, I do."

She moved her hands upward in long strokes along his calves and thighs, rubbing hard, panting. "You feel that, don't you?"

"Yes."

"You're just tense. You've been worrying about old Jasper too much." She moved one long fingernail lightly along the inside of his thigh, into his crotch. "Oh, yes. There's nothing wrong with you that little Emily can't cure."

Later, she lay in the crook of his arm against the white pillows, and they smoked, flicking their ashes into the small glass ashtray resting on Kevin's belly.

"Kevin?"

"Hm?"

"What you thinking?"

"Nothing."

"About old Jasper?"

"No." He turned his head toward her. "You cured that."

"You know, you and Jasper were really something against Castalon last year. Jesus! You ate us up! And that Meskin kid. What's his name?"

"Julio Garcia."

"Yeah. He's the fastest human I've ever seen. He's like the roadrunner in those coyote comedies."

"Yeah."

She giggled. "I'll tell you a secret. My cunt used to get wet when you'd throw the ball to him. Especially on those long passes, when he was way, way down the field behind everybody, you know, and you'd heave the ball down there, and it would just float over his shoulder into his arms. Boy!

133

Watching you two connect was just like fucking. It really did things to me."

"I wish I'd known that at the time."

"Oh, hush! I tried."

"You were too bashful."

"Shit. You just had your nose up in the air all the time."

"Well, it isn't there this year."

"Yeah, that's tough shit. Could you have won District again?"

"Yep."

"And this is your last year, too, ain't it?"

"Yep. And Julio's. And Jasper's."

"Gee, that's tough shit. Look." She pointed toward the window. The dawn was creeping under the lowered shade.

He stroked her blonde curls. "We didn't get much sleep, did we?"

"That's okay. I don't go to work till two o'clock."

"I've got to hit the road sometime."

"You can tell them you slept late."

Three

Kevin hated the funeral. The sweetness of incense, the clang of bells, the chanting of the Mexican priest, the genuflecting and kneeling of all around him while he and Mary Beth remained seated on the hard wooden pew were alien to him. The garish plaster suffering Jesus above the altar, the weeping Virgin and sad, haloed saints in San Ignacio's cheap pictures and statuary reminded him of smaller versions of them that he had seen in the curio shops of Juarez and Ojinaga. Such gimcrackery and superstition he considered even worse than Willie Joe Callahan's list of silly sins and Bible-thumping, ungrammatical hellfire. And at Mountainview Cemetery, while the priest stood among the tombstones of Anglo merchants and cowboys and housewives and sprinkled holy water on the coffin of Emiliano Hawthorne, he concluded that there's no decent way to enter eternity.

Now, as he stood in Carmelita's living room, while Mexicans wept and friends of the Hawthornes heaped food onto plates and passed them to the mourners, some of whom hadn't seen Emiliano since he was a child, disgust welled up within him. Carmelita and Rosa sat apart from the rest, on a small daybed in the corner. Their faces were tear-streaked, but their eyes were dry now. Rosa's face wore a kind of Indian gravity that made her look more Mexican than he had ever seen her. He caught her eye. She whispered into Carmelita's ear. Carmelita gazed at Kevin a long moment, then nodded, and Rosa stood and smoothed her skirt and walked around the circle of weeping, chattering relatives to him. They closed the screen door gently and stood on the small porch, squinting into the sunny afternoon. "Let's go sit in the car," Kevin said. He held the gate open for her, then opened the door of the old Ford, as if she were dressed in an evening gown. He scooted under the steering wheel. "I finally fixed the radio," he said. He flicked it on.

Kyle Kimbrow's nasal whine emerged from the warm-up hum. "Public Health Service figures indicated today that our record outbreak of infantile paralysis is apparently on the wane. But the forty-two thousand three hundred and seventy-two cases reported up to October fourth surpassed the twelve-month total for the previous record year . . ."

Kevin flicked off the radio and stared through the windshield, his left arm draped over the top of the steering wheel. Rosa's head was bowed. Her fingers toyed with the lace on the front of her white blouse. "I still can't believe

135

he's dead," she murmured. "I never believed he would really die."

"I know."

She glanced at him. "No, you don't."

"Hey, Rosa, let's go somewhere."

"Where?"

"Just somewhere else. Where would you like to go?"

"I don't care."

"Where *is* there to go?"

"I don't know. Let's just ride."

He turned the key and pushed the starter button. He turned the car down the dirt road and then into the highway toward town.

"Don't go through town," Rosa said. "Somebody might see us."

"So what?"

"I don't think you want to be seen with me. Alone."

"Oh, shit, Rosa!"

"Please. Let's go the other way."

Kevin swung the car into the parking lot in front of San Ignacio Church and turned it around. They roared back down the hill at the foot of Leaping Panther Mountain. She pointed across Kevin toward Old Fort Appleby. "Let's go in there."

He turned the Ford across the highway and eased it across the rickety old cattle-guard that Carl Birdsong had built long ago, so tourists could drive into his pasture and snap pictures of each other smiling in front of the crumbling buildings. He drove slowly along the narrow dirt road that wound among the ruins, gazing at them as they passed. "I wish I had lived here then," he said.

"My great-grandfather did. Grandpa used to tell me stories about him and the soldiers and the Indians and the stagecoach."

136

"Tell them to me."

"Stop the car."

They got out. She took his hand, intertwining her fingers with his. He looked at her in surprise, but she ignored him. She pointed to an adobe wall standing alone on the stone foundation of what had been a small, rectangular building. "That was the chapel. My great-grandfather hid from the Indians up on the roof of that building."

"Really?"

"Other people were there, too. One of them was Jasper's great-grandfather."

"Aw, come on!"

She grinned slyly. "You think I'm making it up? Other people were up there, too. Guess who one of them was."

"Who?"

"My great-grandmother. Or the woman who would be my great-grandmother. Grandpa says she became my great-grandmother up there."

"In front of the other people?"

Rosa laughed. "Maybe it was a dark night, and she promised not to cry out."

Kevin laughed, too. He kissed her on the cheek. She feigned indignation. "Mr. Adams!"

"Come on. Let's walk down to the grove."

"There are mosquitos down there."

"Not anymore. We took care of them last month."

"Why did you kiss me, Mr. Adams?"

"Because I love you."

She cocked her eyebrow. "Really?"

Kevin reached into the car and pulled a neatly folded Army blanket out of the back seat. They strolled behind the ruins of the enlisted men's barracks, down through the long-sterile trees of the post orchard to the grove of majestic old cottonwoods. A wooden cover had been fitted over the mouth of the stone-lined spring. The bermuda grass in the round, flat space enclosed by the trees was brown and brittle. Kevin spread the blanket near the spring. They lay on their backs and watched the sunlight turn the leaves to silver, listened to the wind turn them into rushing water.

"Look," Rosa said. "The edges of the leaves are yellow."

"Yes. Summer's over."

"Poor Gregorio. All his sons are dead."

"Hush."

She turned. Her blue eyes flickered across his solemn face. "You're right. Let's don't talk about dead people."

"Good."

"Do you really love me?"

"Yes."

"Then make love to me."

He grabbed the edge of the blanket and doubled it over them. His hand moved along her leg. He kissed her.

"Oh, Kevin! I *do* love you!"

His hand moved to her panties, and she lifted her hips as he pulled them down. He pulled the blanket closer about them, then caressed her thigh with long, gentle strokes. Her flesh trembled under his hand.

"Are you sure you want me to?" he asked.

"Yes," she replied. "Do it."

"I *do love* you," he said.

"Do it," she said.

He knelt between her legs, holding the blanket around his shoulders with one hand while the other fumbled with his belt buckle. She raised her hips again and gathered her skirt about her waist. Then, as his body lowered upon her, she clutched him and guided him. Her eyes widened when he entered her.

"Easy," she whispered. "Go slow."

As he slid slowly into her, she grasped his hips with both

hands, then suddenly thrust herself upon him, powerfully. *"Oh!"* she cried, and he felt something tear within her. He stopped.

"Rosa!" he whispered. "What did I do?"

Tears welled in her eyes. She smiled. "You made me a woman, silly."

"Oh, my God!"

She patted his rump. "Don't worry," she said.

"Doesn't it hurt?"

"A little. Kiss me, darling."

As they kissed, she moved her hips, slowly drawing him farther and farther into her. Then he began moving, too.

"Oh, Kevin, it's *good!*" she whispered. "Aren't you glad?"

In Jasper's dream, Kevin handed him the ball. The crowd standing along the sidelines cheered wildly, but he couldn't run. He was in his iron lung. His golden helmet rested on a snow-white pillow. Somehow, he handed the ball back to Kevin. Kevin ran over the goal line, past the goalposts, through the gate where the spectators had entered the schoolgrounds. Suddenly Kevin was on top of Leaping Panther Mountain, running along its crest, dodging rocks and trees. The sun glinted sharply on his helmet. Though he was very far away, Jasper could read the number on his green jersey and see the smile on his face.

Four

When Ginnie would let them, the Eisenbargers spent Sunday afternoons in bed. They took turns persuading the child to stay out of their bedroom, wheedling her to play with her blocks, her dolls, her toy cars, a little longer.

139

Sometimes they would bring her into their bed, and Genevieve would read to her while Jay read the Sunday *El Paso Times.* When Ginnie went down for her nap, they customarily made love. Eisenbarger thought it a waste of time to read the newspaper every day, but making love to Genevieve and reading it on Sunday were pleasant to do while his dough was rising. He made four loaves of bread every Sunday. His father, who boasted that he had never tasted store bread, had taught him. Genevieve was sexy on Sundays. Their bed, holding a night and morning of body heat, became a tumbled nest that appealed to the instinctual side of her nature and warmed away her inhibitions.

He loved Kevin's part in the Sunday ritual, too. He had entered it two years ago, when Eisenbarger had assigned him to write a term paper on "Edgar Allen Poe and the Supernatural." He had come to ask a question about it. While the bread baked, they talked about Poe. Their conversation was the first about books that Eisenbarger had had since leaving Houston. He invited the boy to linger and share the bread and cheese and jelly and the strong black coffee. Afterwards, while Genevieve was curled up on the sofa with an Agatha Christi, Kevin helped Eisenbarger do the dishes, and they droned into Dickens and Shakespeare and Shelley and Byron and other novelists and poets that Eisenbarger got up at five o'clock to read before he dressed and drove to school.

Eisenbarger felt something awakening in the boy that evening. He discovered in him a sharp hunger for ideas, for beauty. He saw in him the *tabula rasa* he had read about in the education textbooks, an empty vessel waiting to be filled, a diamond-in-the-rough awaiting the love and skill of the master stonecutter. In six years as a teacher, Eisenbarger had known no other student who thought literature was important and was struggling to understand why. At midnight Eisenbarger lent Kevin three of his prized Heritage Club editions. *David Copperfield, The Three Musketeers, The Song of Roland.* Afterwards, his generosity amazed him, and bothered him a little. He wouldn't have entrusted those immaculate volumes even to Genevieve, had she been interested in reading them. But Kevin proved worthy of the trust. He read them, even *The Song of Roland,* and returned them undamaged, and was eager to talk about them. He borrowed many books after that.

That spring, Eisenbarger encouraged Kevin to enter the district interscholastic essay-writing contest, and he won. He won the regional competition, too, and placed second in the state contest at the University of Texas. He returned full of pride and desire to be a writer. The Sunday sessions became more exhilarating for both of them.

Eisenbarger was glad to hear the knock. Genevieve rolled over and opened her eyes. "It's probably Kevin," he said. "Don't get up." Genevieve grunted and closed her eyes. Eisenbarger laid aside the newspaper and covered his nakedness with his old gray robe and slipped his feet into his fleece-lined slippers. He padded down the hall, pulling Ginnie's door closed on the way, and shoved back the bolt on the front door.

Kevin grinned. "I hope I'm not interrupting anything."

"No. Come in. Ginnie and Genevieve are asleep." He waved toward the kitchen.

Kevin pulled a chair from under the small breakfast table and sat down. "If I get to be a pain, I hope you'll tell me."

Eisenbarger shook his head. "Start the water while I put on some clothes."

Kevin filled a saucepan at the sink and put it on the burner. He found the canister and spooned the rich-smelling coffee into the basket of the drip pot. In a few minutes, Eisenbarger reappeared, tucking the tail of a khaki shirt into his Levis. He tossed a pack of cigarettes and a box of matches on the table. "Take one if you want."

Kevin lit up, and so did Eisenbarger. "Well, Kevin, how goes it?"

"The same. And with you?"

"The same, also. I heard you saw Jasper."

"I wish I hadn't."

"It was a good thing to do, though."

"I didn't imagine it would be so horrible."

Eisenbarger exhaled the gray smoke and poured the boiling water into the pot. "What are you reading these days?"

"Nothing. I haven't read anything since school was shut down."

"Why not?"

"I start reading, and my mind slips away from me, and I get nervous and have to get up and try to do something. The trouble is, there's nothing to do. Except go to funerals. Three funerals, Mr. Jay. Four people I've known, in three weeks. Has that ever happened in Fort Appleby before?"

"Not since the Indian days, I guess."

"Doesn't it scare you?"

"It did at first, but it doesn't now."

"I don't mean, does it scare you that you might die. I mean, doesn't it scare you that so many *others* are dying."

"Wait a minute. Let me check the bread." Eisenbarger padded into the living room and returned carrying a large mixing bowl covered with a dishtowel. He clutched a thin brown volume under his arm. He gave the book to Kevin, then carried the bowl to the drainboard. He punched down the dough with his fist and dumped it onto the floured surface. "Pour us some coffee," he said.

Kevin laid the book on the table and got down two white cups and saucers from the cabinet and filled them. *"The*

Meditations of Marcus Aurelius," he said. "Is that what you're reading?"

"I have been, yes."

"It doesn't sound very exciting."

"It isn't. Unless you're asking the questions that you're asking me."

"What questions?"

Eisenbarger pulled his dough into four hunks, shaped them into small loaves, and placed them carefully into the pans. Then he wiped his hands with a towel and took a long pull on his coffee. "Good and strong. I taught you well." He carried the cup to the table and set it down, and took the little volume from Kevin's hands. He opened it and turned the pages carefully. Then he read: " 'Death is such as generation is, a mystery of nature; a composition out of the same elements, and a decomposition into the same; and altogether not a thing of which any man should be ashamed, for it is not contrary to the nature of a reasonable animal, and not contrary to the reason of our constitution.' " He peered at Kevin over his glasses. "Do you know what that means?"

"I think he means that everybody dies, nobody knows why, but it's the natural thing to do."

Eisenbarger smiled. "Not bad. Try this one: 'Time is like a river made up of the events which happen, and a violent stream; for as soon as a thing has been seen, it is carried away, and another comes in its place, and this will be carried away, too.' " He peered at Kevin again.

"I think that means that nothing lasts very long, and that whatever takes its place doesn't last long, either."

"Exactly."

Ginnie cried out, and there was a squeak of springs in the

143

bedroom. "Jay! Get her!" Genevieve called. "I'll be out in a minute."

"Okay, honey!" Eisenbarger closed the book and laid it on the table and disappeared out the door. He returned quickly, carrying the child. "Look who's here, Ginnie," he cooed. She lifted her head and gazed at Kevin, crossly, then smiled and held out her arms to him. He took her and set her on his knee.

"Kev! Play top!"

"Okay, Ginnie." He carried her to the living room, where her big steel top lay on the floor. He set her on the rug and pumped the top until its merry-go-round decorations blurred and it began to whistle. Ginnie laughed. He kept her occupied with the top until Genevieve walked into the room, pulling a pink comb through her long brown hair.

"Hello, Kevin. Long time, no see."

"Yeah."

"I'll take her now. It's time for her dinner. Will you stay? It's the usual Eisenbarger Sunday Night Special."

"Why do you think I came?"

She smiled and pulled her green sweater toward her thin hips. "Jay, is the bread in the oven?"

"No, but it won't be long."

"Well, pour Kevin some coffee and come in here. I've got to feed Ginnie."

Eisenbarger balanced the two cups on their saucers and clutched Marcus Aurelius under his arm. He set them on the coffee table and sat down beside Kevin on the sofa.

"It could have been Ginnie instead of Juanito Rodriguez," Kevin said out of the blue. Then he was embarrassed. "All I meant was, how would you have handled it?"

Eisenbarger flipped the little brown volume open again and leafed carefully through it. Then he read, " 'Be like the promontory against which the waves continually break, but

144

it stands firm and tames the fury of the waves around it.' "

"Could you have done that?"

"I don't know. I hope I would have tried. A professor of mine said Marcus wrote that right after his daughter died. Or was it his wife? I don't remember."

"He was a helluva guy."

"Apparently. The Romans declared him a god when he died."

"Time didn't entirely carry him away, did it?"

"No. He left a good book, which I hope you'll do someday, too."

Later, when Ginnie was asleep again and the bread was ready, Eisenbarger sliced it, and they ate it hot, with butter dripping off it, with lots of cheese and grape jelly and black coffee. Then Kevin borrowed the *Meditations* and carried it with him. He called Carmelita from the phone booth at the Gulf station.

She could see the moon through the filthy windowpanes. She was stretched naked on a ragged, dusty quilt that she had spread over an old mattress in her storeroom. The storeroom was the woodshed long ago. It was away from the house, at the back edge of the yard, and she was delighted when she discovered the mattress there. She had come to pull out Rosa's crib, to give it to Elena Mendoza. The mattress was behind it, leaning against the wall. She laid it on the floor and spread the quilt over it, and it became her trysting place. She felt safer there, away from the house, away from Rosa and the possibility of a squeaking spring or a cry awakening her. She even enjoyed the strong odor of the dust mixed with the musk of their lovemaking. The woodshed smelled like the lair of animals in heat, a scent appropriate to their kind of loving.

She looked at the boy next to her, asleep. His skin was

silver in the moonlight, and the position of his body reminded her of an animal running. Some quick, lean animal. A deer or a greyhound. Had he kept his promise? He had collected on his bargain often enough, and never, even in his rare talkative moods, had he mentioned Rosa. Or any other girl.

Carmelita smiled. She could imagine no more satisfactory arrangement. She, widowed and in her prime; he, young and strong, inexperienced, eager to learn. What a ferocious lover he was! She had learned to like his ferocity. She thought she understood it now. She almost wished that after she had thoroughly trained him, tamed him just a little, she could present him to her daughter. But he would marry some sweet *gringo* virgin who would be terrified of him. He would cruise alleys at night. Well, if he came down *her* alley . . .

She poked her elbow into his ribs. "Wake up."

He rolled onto his back and yawned. "What time is it?"

"Almost midnight. You'd better go."

He nestled his head on her breasts. His tongue flicked one of her nipples. It sprang erect.

"Kevin, stop it!"

"One more time."

"No. If you don't get home, your mother's going to ask questions, and you'll lie, and she won't believe you, and she'll check your bed every night."

Kevin groaned.

"Get out of here."

He got up and fumbled with his clothing in the moonlight. She lay back on the mattress, watching him dress, enjoying her great calm and the smell of herself.

Five

By mid-October, when the oaks and the cottonwoods burst into autumn flame, the hot reality of summer had faded out of mind. The death of Juanito Rodriguez and Emiliano Hawthorne and Ada Lou and Kathleen Callahan paled from community catastrophe to family tragedy, and finally to personal misfortune. The National Foundation for Infantile Paralysis announced that there were fifty-five thousand polio victims in America so far in 1952, double the toll of 1951. Fort Appleby felt a common bond with cities and states far away. Reading the statistics, the citizens nodded knowingly. Yes, they knew how it is. They were there. They were part of it. But Amy Ferguson's predictions of Armageddon were delivered less and less frequently, and then not at all. The drought resumed its old place as the chief topic of conversation. The men hunched over the coffee cups at the drugstore knew it was too late to wish for more rain, so they hoped for a heavy snowfall.

At Hendricks Memorial Hospital, Jasper was rolled into an ambulance and driven to the Abilene airport, where he was carried aboard a private plane. Carl and Vera Birdsong accompanied him to Gonzales, in South Texas, where, they had been told, Jasper might learn to use his legs again. They smiled and patted his hand. A doctor had told them he hadn't expected Jasper to survive. "The boy has guts," he said. At Gonzales, Jasper was assigned a room near Sue Ann Perkins, who had been there two weeks already. Sue Ann, Daisy told the Birdsongs, was learning to walk again. Jasper was surprised to hear that the little girl was from Fort Appleby, and that the school janitor's grandson had

147

died. He wondered if he had ever seen Juanito. He couldn't remember.

Gladys Evans, secretary to the Fort Appleby Board of Education, wrote a letter. "Dear Parent," it said.

"The Board of Education of the Fort Appleby Independent School District has decided that all classes should resume on Monday, October 20, 1952. No certified case of infantile paralysis has occurred in the community since September 10, and that fact, plus the cooler fall weather that we are experiencing, encourages us to believe that our epidemic has run its course. In any case, we feel there is little to be gained by further suspension of the school year.

"Obviously, the school term must be extended into the summer to make up for the time we have lost. Just how far into the summer has not yet been determined. The Board of Education will keep you informed of future developments.

"The Board grieves with those who have lost loved ones, and thanks God that the epidemic seems to have ended."

There was a festive air about the day. Locker doors were banged with abandon. Students shouted their greetings to one another. Their laughter was loud and raucous. Eisenbarger stood at the intersection of the corridors, swinging his paddle as of old. But he touched no one with it. He was smiling, too. This day, this new beginning, had convinced them all that the thing which they had feared had passed them by. The shadow of calamity in which they had lived for more than five weeks had disappeared. The Board of Education had decreed them safe. A few students and teachers said words of sympathy to Rosa Hawthorne and Eduardo Rodriguez and the surviving Callahan children, but they were whispered and brief and were received in self-conscious silence. Rosa and Eduardo and the Callahans were as ready as the rest to shove their grief into a private corner and resume the normal way of things. It was good to see, as Eisenbarger had, Celestino Gomez touch Cora Aguilar's tightly sweatered breast in the library and to say nothing, this once. It was good to walk into the boys' restroom and see the blue-gray clouds of cigarette smoke rising from the latched toilet stalls and not knock on the doors with the paddle. There would be time enough another day for rules and discipline. Eisenbarger let the boys take their time preening their flat-tops and duck-tails before the mirrors. Water slid down their temples like sweat. He smiled privately to the blackboard when he chalked up his homework assignments and heard his students groan. Even phoning to check on the few absentees was a pleasure, for all were absent only because their parents hadn't received, or hadn't opened, or couldn't read the school board's letter.

Eisenbarger was making his last call when George Wilson set the tall trophy on his desk. It was a fluted brass pedestal with a small brass quarterback standing on top, his left arm extended, his right arm cocked to throw the small brass football. The plaque at the base of the column was engraved.

FORT APPLEBY HIGH SCHOOL
CHAMPIONS
District 3, Class B
Six-Man Football
1952

Eisenbarger glanced at Wilson, then gazed at the trophy until he completed the call. As he hung up, his eyes returned to Wilson's. "Well," he said.

"They mailed it to me."

"The season isn't over yet."

"No. We still have three games on our schedule."

Wilson sat down on the small wooden chair by Eisenbarger's desk and ran his fingers over the short bristles of his crew cut.

"I guess they still don't want to play you," Eisenbarger said.

"We would have lost. They know that. We wouldn't have won the trophy if they had played us."

Eisenbarger leaned back and rocked slowly in his swivel chair. The angles of the tall trophy gleamed in the sunlight streaming through the open window behind him. "What are you going to do with it?" he asked.

Wilson's brow furrowed. "I didn't mean to accept it. They never mailed it before. They always presented it at the coaches' meeting at the end of the season. I was going to turn it down."

"It's already engraved," Eisenbarger said.

"Yeah. They never did that before, either. The winning school always had to have its own name engraved on it."

"I guess they want you to keep it."

"It's spite, Jay. They're pissed off because I wouldn't forfeit. They're sticking it up my ass."

"Could be."

Wilson's eyes dropped. His hands were in his lap, their fingers intertwined. He rotated his thumbs, one around the other, first the left around the right, then the right around the left, watching them. "Do you think I did right?"

"Any of them might have done the same thing under the circumstances."

Wilson sighed. He pulled himself to his feet. "Well, have Eduardo put it in the case. I don't think we need to call an assembly to present it to the boys."

"What are you going to do about the bi-district game?"

"I think I'll write and thank them for the trophy and tell them that the runner-up should represent us at bi-district."

Eisenbarger nodded. "I think that's a good idea."

"You think it is?"

"Yes. I think it's a wise decision."

The coach stepped toward the door, then turned. "Jay, has Fort Appleby ever fired a coach for having a losing season?"

"Not that I know of."

"It's not a bad town, is it? A fellow could really settle down here, couldn't he?"

"Yes. I intend to, anyway."

Wilson pulled the door shut behind him. Eisenbarger gazed at the trophy for a long time, then picked it up.

Eduardo had shoved all the desks to the walls and was mopping the floor in the science lab. He straightened himself as Eisenbarger appeared in the doorway. "The children spilled a lot of stuff today," he said.

"They're a little rambunctious, I guess. They were away so long."

"Yes. It's all right."

Eisenbarger held out the trophy. "Will you take care of this?"

Eduardo wiped his hands on his overalls and accepted the trophy. He cradled it gently and read the engraved words. "Yes," he said. "I'll find a special place for this one."

DECEMBER, 1952

One

Mary Beth Mallory married James B. Adams in a hotel room in Dallas on Christmas Day, 1934. The doctor had told her only five days before that she was pregnant. She expected it to be the most miserable Christmas of her life, but it wasn't. Jim wanted to marry her. He was even glad that she was pregnant. He said he was, anyway. It was a cold day. The justice of the peace didn't even take off his overcoat. He stood beside the bed, read rapidly from his little book, slammed it shut, signed the marriage license, and held out his hand for his fee. Then he and his two witnesses were gone. It was over so quickly that Mary Beth wasn't sure she was really married until the license was duly recorded in the big book at the Dallas County Courthouse.

Kevin was only six months old when they came to Fort Appleby. Mary Beth dreaded the move away from the city to the edge of nowhere. But Jim wanted his own insurance agency. There was none in Davis County. Davis County was a fertile field, never plowed, Jim said. He was right. They prospered. Then came the war and the draft. By the time the telegram came, Mary Beth knew the business. She had the business, and Kevin, but no more Jim. She came across his signature on old letters in the files sometimes, and she had a few snapshots, and his ghost came back to her at Christmastime. She remembered him holding the sprig of mistletoe over her head beside the bed in the hotel room. "A kiss won't do," he said.

The memory brought a slight smile to her lips. She was reclining on the sofa, her horn-rimmed glasses perched on

155

the bridge of her nose. In her lap, in the bright light of the reading lamp, lay a needlepoint chair cover that she was making for Carmelita for Christmas. She glanced at Kevin. From certain angles he looked like Jim. He hunched over the desk at the other end of the living room, his own lamp casting a glare across his homework binder. He looked like Jim now. Jim hunched like that when he was working.

Kevin turned. "Mother?"

"Hm?"

He dropped his pen and clasped his hands tightly together, then drew a deep breath, letting the air escape slowly. "May I take Rosa to the dance?"

"What, Kevin?"

"I want to take Rosa to the dance. Is it okay with you?"

She pulled off her glasses. "Are you asking my permission to date a *Mexican?*"

"I want to take Rosa to the Christmas dance," he said quietly. "That's all."

"That's *all?*" Now her voice was high, whinny. "You want to nuzzle a Mexican in public, and you say that's *all?*"

"I'm talking about *Rosa!*" Kevin was shouting. He had planned not to.

"You're talking about a *greaser tamale!*" She folded her arms across her breasts and shuddered. She squinted at her son, calmer now, ashamed. "I didn't mean that. I'm sorry. Rosa's a good girl. But there are things we don't do."

"I *know* there are things we don't do. I just don't see why we *shouldn't.*"

"If you don't know, I can't tell you." She put on her glasses and picked up the needlepoint. "The answer is no."

"Why?"

"Don't ask me again."

"It doesn't make sense."

"Don't ask me again."

156

Kevin got up and stalked to the coathooks beside the door. He grabbed his heavy mackinaw and rammed his arm into the sleeve.

"Where do you think you're going?" Mary Beth said.

"None of your goddamn business."

Two

Kevin zipped up his jacket and walked around the car to open the door. "You'd better put on your coat," he said. "It's pretty cold."

Alicia Jones, glowing white above her royal-blue strapless gown, pulled Jasper's letter-jacket around her shoulders. She smiled up at Kevin. "I'd better be careful with my corsage. It's so pretty."

The corsage was red rosebuds. Kevin had driven to Sharon for it late in the afternoon and delivered it to Alicia's mother, who exclaimed over his thoughtfulness, his taste, his gallantry. Kevin blushed later, when Alicia, in the presence of her mother, asked him to pin the corsage on her dress and designated the V of her bodice as its nesting place. Mrs. Jones smiled indulgently while Kevin fumbled with the flowers and the pin in the narrow, perfumed space.

Inside the gymnasium, Jim Burnett and the Pecos River Boys were tuning up on the sideline of the basketball court. The crowd was already large. Men in shiny boots and western suits smelling of mothballs and cleaning fluid stood in clusters on the hardwood floor, chatting with women in net-covered formals and new permanent waves. They occasionally stepped back for Eduardo Rodriguez, who was broadcasting powdered wax over the glossy surface. In the corner by the concession stand, men with gray hair and large bellies were staking claim to places at the folding

157

tables and uncorking pints of Heaven Hill and Early Times. Elmer Martin, behind a gray steel cashbox open on a table near the door, leered when Kevin lifted the green-and-gold jacket from Alicia's shoulders and hung it on the rack. "You're a couple, I guess. You sure don't look stag."

"That's right."

"Five dollars, then."

Kevin counted one-dollar bills onto the table. Martin smiled at Alicia. "If I was thirty years younger, I'd make you forget this young squirt."

Alicia wrinkled her nose. "Thank you, Mr. Martin. If Kevin tuckers out, maybe we can have a turn together."

Martin smiled ruefully and shook his head. "It won't do for me to try to keep up with the young bucks. My wild oats have been sown, threshed, and hauled to the barn."

Alicia giggled. "More's the pity, Mr. Martin."

She took Kevin's arm. They moved to the sideline of the court and looked over the crowd, searching out people their own age, waving greetings. Willie Joe Callahan limped up wearing his pearl-handled revolver. "I'll expect you in church tomorrow," he said.

"You're going to preach against dancing. I've already heard it," Kevin replied.

"Well, it didn't take, did it? I might say a word or two about drinking, too. Maybe you'd be interested in that?"

"I haven't had a drop, preacher."

Callahan sneered. "Say that tomorrow with a straight face. We're having a baptism. I'd like a good crowd."

"Who got saved?"

"Mrs. Perkins." He tipped his hat to Alicia and limped away, just as Clay Sanger slapped Kevin hard across the back.

"Hey, what did the sky pilot want? Warning you about

coveting your neighbor's ass?" Sweat shone in beads on his forehead and upper lip.

"Been hitting the hootch, haven't you?" Kevin said.

"Yeah, I waited too long to get a date. Maybe I'll just *take* one." He pinched Alicia's cheek.

"Get your sweaty hands off of me, Sanger! You'll ruin my makeup!"

"That isn't all I'd like to ruin!"

"Keep talking like that, and Kevin will whip your ass, won't you, Kevin? You'll puke gin for a week."

Clay smiled at Kevin. "Could you do it, skinny fart?"

"Yeah."

"Shit! I outweigh you forty pounds."

"I'm fast and dirty. You better believe it."

"You talking about fighting or fucking?"

"Shut up, shitmouth!" Alicia hissed. "You've got the filthiest mind in town."

Clay grinned slyly and whispered in Alicia's ear. "Bet you wish old Jasper was here."

Kevin grabbed Clay's collar and pulled his face close to his. "One more word and I'll cut your throat. You'd better believe me."

"Turn loose," Clay whispered, glancing around him.

"Do you *believe* me?"

"I'm not up to fighting you tonight, Adams."

"Well, just name your time."

"I didn't mean to make you mad."

Kevin released him, and he walked quickly to the concession stand. He leaned back against the counter and glared back across the floor.

Jim Burnett, resplendent in red boots and snow-white suit with "Pecos River Boys" emblazoned in red sequins across the shoulders, pushed his hat back from his forehead. "Good evening, ladies and gentlemen," he said into the microphone. "It's a pleasure to be in Fort Appleby tonight. It's for such a worthy cause. More than fifty thousand Americans got polio this year. You folks don't have to be told what that means. Your being here shows you're willing to fight. Nearly every penny you spend is going to the March of Dimes. You've already paid your money to get in, and most of that goes to the March of Dimes. The money you spend at the concession stand does, too. So eat and drink a lot. And on the sidelines you see several nail kegs set up. Just drop something into one of those as you dance by. A nickel, a dime, a quarter, a dollar. Whatever you can afford. It's for a worthy cause. Me and the boys, we're going to start things off now with that great Ernest Tubb tune, 'I'd Waltz Across Texas with You.' "

Alicia moved into the circle of Kevin's arms. He was sorry that the band had begun with a waltz. He didn't waltz well, and he moved with uncertainty. But it didn't matter. Alicia, after the first few steps, moved closer and laid her head on his shoulder.

"You're tall. I never realized how much taller you are than Jasper."

"Yeah."

"You smell good. What's that you've got on?"

"Old Spice."

"Umm. It smells so *good.*"

"You smell good, too. What are *you* wearing?"

"White Shoulders. You like it?"

"Umm-hmm. You've got the whitest shoulders I ever saw."

She licked the lobe of his ear. "Devil! The first dance, and you're trying to seduce me!"

When the waltz was finished, the band swung immediately into the hellbent rhythm of "Under the Double

Eagle," and Kevin was swinging Alicia so fast and in circles so tight that a real dance step was impossible. All that mattered was the wild, quickening whine of fiddle and steel guitar, the warmth of flesh and hair against flesh and hair, the musk of perfume and sweat. Dancers bumped each other, laughed, and moved deeper into the dizzying whirl of music and color and booze and perfume. When the music stopped at last and Jim Burnett laughed into the microphone, Alicia pulled Kevin to her. "Hold me, Kevin, or I'll fall for sure."

He hugged her. "Let's get a drink. I'm about to die."

They walked along the wall toward the concession stand. Four wreaths of plastic holly were hanging over the bench where the substitutes sat during basketball games. In the center of the first was a photograph of Sue Ann Perkins, sitting on Sam Perkins's lap on the steps of their trailer. In the next, Emiliano Hawthorne smiled from the back of a pinto pony. In the third, Juanito Rodriguez sat on a rug, holding a ball, laughing. In the last, Bob Hope smiled down into the face of Jasper Birdsong in an iron lung. It was the skeleton of Jasper that Kevin had seen at the hospital. Under the wreaths, foot-high red letters spelled out:

REMEMBER THEM AND GIVE

Alicia stared at Bob Hope and Jasper. "Jesus, he's changed! Kevin, it's awful!"

"Yeah, I guess he'll be different from now on."

"What do you think he'll be like?"

"There's no way to know."

"Will he expect me to love him when he gets back?"

"I don't know. Do you love him now?"

She lifted his hand and kissed it. "Would you think I was awful if I said I don't know?"

161

"No. I'm sort of sorry, though."

"So am I." Then she brightened. "Come on. Let's don't think about serious things tonight. Where's that drink?"

He bought two Cokes and wrapped paper napkins around the cold, wet bottles. "Let's take them to the car," he said. "I've got a bottle out there."

"Oh, good."

Kevin took Jasper's jacket from the hanger and draped it around her shoulders.

"Where you going? The dancing's barely started," Elmer Martin said.

"We need a little fresh air."

"That ain't all that'll be fresh out there, I bet."

They walked into the night. The wind hit their sweaty skins like ice. She held the Cokes and shivered while he helped her into the car. He got in and started the engine. The blast from the heater was cold, too. "It'll warm up in a minute," he said. He flicked on the radio and turned the knob until he found soft, big-band music. He reached under the seat and pulled out the bourbon, still sealed and new in its small paper bag. "Drink down your Coke a little." He guzzled half of his, broke the seal on the bourbon and filled the Coke bottle to the top. She handed him hers. He held it up to the light and poured with care.

"You make stiff ones," she said.

"It's a cold night."

"Yes, it is." She burrowed under his arm, hugging the jacket to her. "I wish the heater would get warm." She tilted her head, and he kissed her. She opened her mouth slightly, and darted her tongue into his. They moved slowly beyond a kiss, into a languid physical communion that isolated them from the airline commercial on the radio and the drumming of the Ford's old V-8 at the edge of their consciousness. At last, she broke the kiss and pecked him lightly on the lips. "Old Kevin's not bad."

"Alicia's not bad, either."

"I don't need this anymore." She pulled the jacket from her shoulders and tossed it into the back seat. She curled her legs under her and straightened the long, netted skirt. She reclined across Kevin's lap and rested her head in the crook of his arm. She sipped the drink.

"Whew! That's strong!"

"You'll get used to it. We'll dance better."

"Umm."

The late-great Glenn Miller played "String of Pearls." She hummed a bar or two. They drank slowly, finished together and tossed the bottles into the back floorboard.

"Hmph." She smiled wryly.

"What?"

"I was just thinking, I lost my cherry in this car. Back there." She arched her wrist toward the back seat.

"I know."

"Boys do talk, don't they?"

"Jasper's my best friend."

"I wasn't complaining."

"How was it?"

"Jasper was scared to death. He lasted about five seconds. It must have been his first time, too."

The streetlight outside the gymnasium cast the shadow of the steering wheel across her face, but he could see her gazing up at him. "What are you thinking?" she asked. "Your face is in the dark."

"Nothing. Well, about fucking, I guess."

She picked up his hand and moved it to her breast. His fingers touched a hoop of wire.

"Merry Widow," she said. "About fifty hooks and eyes."

"Jesus."

"Don't worry. I'm not wearing panties. I'm ready for you, Kevin Adams."

He kissed her fiercely. His hand tugged at the long skirt. She pulled away. "You'll tear my dress." She straightened her legs and lifted her hips. She carefully worked the skirt upward until her middle was engulfed in net. Then she relaxed and laid his hand on her thigh. "There," she said.

He kissed her again. His hand moved quickly up her thigh, past the top of her stocking and the clasps of the garter straps, to the hair and moisture between her legs.

She gasped. "See? I told you I was ready. Do you have a rubber?"

"Yes."

"Get it." She sat up and moved to her side of the seat. Her dress circled her waist like a dark cloud. Her white thighs and hips glowed above the stocking tops.

He took the rubber from his wallet and rolled it on. He slid across the seat. "I should tell you that I don't love you," he said.

"I know." She straddled him on her knees and moved down upon him. He held the long dress out of their way.

As they moved onto the dance floor and he took her into his arms again, she said softly, "I know who you *do* love, Kevin Adams."

"Who?"

"Rosa Hawthorne."

"What makes you think so?"

"The way you look at her. The way she looks at you. Don't worry. Your secret's safe with me. If it can *be* a secret."

"You're just guessing."

"If you say so."

They moved into the dance. She laid her head on his shoulder. He asked, "What if you were right?"

"I'd say you're in for trouble."

He thought of his mother while they danced, and then of Rosa, and of the other dance, in Little Juarez. He wondered if she was dancing, or out in a car.

Three

Daisy Perkins brushed her long hair. It was still damp. She hummed the hymn that the congregation had sung just before Willie Joe baptized her.

> *I need thee, oh, I need thee,*
> *Every hour I need thee . . .*

Her eye caught Sam's photograph in the gold frame on her dressing table. She turned it away and smiled at herself in the mirror. She was beautiful, even with wet hair. She saw that. And it was good to be naked under the nylon negligee. Her skin felt so alive, so sensitive to the caress of the smooth cloth. Was it the Holy Spirit that made her so alive, so happy? Or was it that the water in the baptistry had been so cold? Would a cold shower have done as well? Whatever it was, she was glad of it. It was so good to be away from hospitals and nurses and therapists. Born again. That's what Willie Joe said she was. She believed it. She felt it. A new life. Starting over.

The knock startled her. "Who is it?"

"Brother Callahan."

She smiled at herself again, and grabbed a lipstick from the mirror top of her table. "Come on in, preacher. I'll be right with you." She hurried with the lipstick, the powder, the rouge. She jumped up and stepped toward the closet, then turned and glanced into the mirror again and smiled again. She wrapped the negligee tightly around her and pulled the sash tight. She shoved her feet into high-heeled slippers with fuzzy balls on top and went into the living room.

Callahan wore his blue preaching suit. He stood just inside the door, his overcoat over his arm, his good hand clasping his crippled one. His eyes widened slightly when he saw her.

"Sit down, preacher. Make yourself comfortable." He sat down quickly in the chair beside the door. She sat down across the room from him.

"The trailers are gone," he said. "The road crew has left."

"Yes. They finished the job and left."

"Where's your husband?"

"He left, too."

Callahan looked puzzled.

"He left for good. He wrote me at Gonzales. Couldn't take it anymore, he said, especially Sue Ann's illness, so he left. Left with the crew."

Callahan's mouth dropped open. "But what about *you?* What are you going to do?"

"Divorce him. What else? And look for a job, I guess, when Sue Ann gets out. He said he was still going to support us, but I sure got to laugh at *that!*"

Callahan's good hand moved to the breast pocket of his coat and touched the purple ribbon marker of the small New Testament he carried there.

"Is this a business call, preacher?"

He flushed. "Well, I was *surprised* when you wrote me that you wanted to be baptized . . . I'd been praying for you, of course. But I didn't expect . . . Well, I usually talk to people

166

before I baptize them, but in your case . . . I just thought I'd come by and talk with you or pray with you or something. I didn't know your husband . . ."

"I wanted you to baptize me because you're a good man, and I reckon your way's probably best. I did a lot of thinking, and praying, too, in Abilene and Gonzales. All those hours . . ."

Callahan was still puzzled, but he nodded. "I wanted to thank you for what you did for me, too . . . You know, that night. It was a foolish, ungodly thing I was about to do. I wasn't thinking right. I wanted you to know that."

Daisy smiled sympathetically. "I know that. We've been through a hard thing. Your wife, she was a good woman, wasn't she?"

"The best. We rode up a rough trail together, and she never complained."

"How are you making it, now that she's . . . gone?"

"Barely. Just barely."

She crossed her legs, then uncrossed them when the negligee fell away from her legs. Her mood had changed. She still felt alive, happy, but the preacher's discomfort and his obvious misery touched her. She suddenly wanted to do something Christian for him.

"Fort Appleby," she said, "it's a pretty town. Is it a *good* town? Are the people friendly?"

"Not very. They've always seemed a little snobbish to me, like they thought they were a little better than most. A little high and mighty."

"Why don't you leave?"

He shrugged. "Six . . . five kids to support. I got two jobs, and I do okay. I'm not the most brilliant preacher in the world. Not the best educated. I can't complain. This town has treated me all right."

"I don't reckon I could find a job here."

167

"I doubt it."

She gazed at him appraisingly, toying with the end of the nylon sash. "Who takes care of your kids for you?"

"I do. The two oldest are some help."

"Why don't you get yourself a Meskin maid?"

"Can't afford it."

They fell silent. She continued to gaze at him, but he refused to meet her eyes.

"Would you like to pray?" he asked at last.

"No."

"Oh."

"Preacher, I'll make you a deal. I'll be your housekeeper for meals and round-trip bus fare to Gonzales every two weeks. Just for a while. Just until me and Sue Ann can get things straightened out."

Now he stared at her. "Mrs. Perkins, I . . . The rumors . . ."

"I'm not offering to *live* with you, preacher, just be your maid! I'll live here in my trailer and just come to your house in the morning like a Meskin. We both need help, and we can help each other. Ain't that what Christianity's all about? What do you say?"

He frowned, and stared at the wall above her head. Then suddenly he rose and stuck out his good left hand. "Well. Just for awhile," he said.

She shook his hand. "Okay. Why don't you stay for Sunday dinner? I was about to fix myself a grilled cheese."

Four

Rosa found him at his locker. "Maybe you could take my books," he said. "I have basketball practice."

Her fingers toyed with the silver crucifix on a thin silver

168

chain around her neck. "I have to talk to you, Kevin."

"What is it?"

Locker doors were slamming around them. Students hurried to reach the front door and the end of the day. "I can't tell you here."

"Rosa, what *is* it?"

"Let's go somewhere else."

"I'm in a hurry."

"In the auditorium. On the stage. No one is in there."

"Well, okay."

"Bring your books. I'll take them home for you."

She turned and disappeared around the corner of the corridor to the Anglo elementary wing and the entrance to the auditorium. Kevin waited, then picked up his books and made his way through the throng of small children in the hallway to the closed glass doors. He glanced around to make sure no teacher was watching, then opened one of the doors, stepped inside and closed it softly.

The auditorium was gloomy and cold. His bootheels thudded on the stone floor, faintly echoing off the empty seats. The green velvet curtain of the stage was closed. He stopped at the foot of the steps to the stage. "Rosa?"

"Here."

He climbed the steps, parted the curtain and stepped into darkness. "I can't see you," he said.

Her breath was on his cheek, then her light kiss. He stooped and laid his books on the floor, then his hands found her. She was trembling. "What's the matter?" he asked.

"I'm in trouble."

His hand found her short hair. She laid her head on his shoulder. "What kind of trouble?"

"Oh, Kevin!"

"What, Rosa? What is it? Tell me!"

169

She pulled his head down and whispered so softly that he couldn't make out her words.

"What?"

"I'm going to have a baby!" she said aloud.

For what seemed an eternity, he could think of nothing to say. He just held her, listening to her sob. At last, he asked, "How do you know?"

"I've missed two periods."

"Can that mean something else?"

Her head shook. "I've always been regular before. Like a clock."

Now Kevin trembled, too. He pulled her tighter into his embrace. "Rosa?" He wished he could see her. He could make out nothing on the stage but the ghostly bulk of a grand piano. "Rosa, am I the father?"

"Bastard!" She jerked away from him.

"I had to ask."

"Under the cottonwoods, bastard!"

"Okay."

"Okay what?" She wasn't sobbing now.

"I don't know."

"What are we going to do?"

"I don't know."

He felt her soft hair against his neck again. "Do you love me?" she asked.

"You know I do."

"Even now? After this?"

"Yes."

"We could have been careful."

"Yes."

"We were careful the other times."

"Yes."

"Why weren't we then?"

"I don't know."

"What are we going to do?"

"I don't know."

"Will you marry me, Kevin?"

"Yes."

"You don't have to."

"I will."

"Do you *want* to marry me, Kevin?"

"Yes, I want to marry you."

"I don't want you to if you don't want to."

"I want to."

She lifted her face. He kissed her. "I *do* want to marry you," he said.

"I'll make you very happy."

"I'll make *you* happy, too."

"We have to tell our mothers."

"I know."

"How will we do that?"

"I don't know. Let me think about it."

"It has to be soon."

"I know."

She squeezed his arm. "I love you *so* much."

"And I love you."

"You know what?"

"What?"

"I'm not crying anymore."

"Good."

"I'm happy, Kevin. Are you happy?"

"Yes, I'm happy."

"Good. Give me your books. You're late for practice."

He picked up the books and handed them to her. "I'll go first," she said. She parted the curtain. "Oh!" She almost collided with Eduardo. He was standing at the top of the steps. She glanced over her shoulder, her eyes wide, frightened.

He held a large cardboard box. Strands of tinsel and loops of metallic red rope dripped over the edge. He thrust it toward her. "The Christmas tree. On the stage."

She squeezed past him and fled up the aisle.

Kevin groped to the curtain and parted it. Eduardo thrust the box toward him. "Excuse me," Kevin said.

Eduardo waited until after nine o'clock to call Carmelita. "I wouldn't tell you if I wasn't a Rodriguez and you weren't a Hawthorne," he said. He had been about to mount the steps of the stage, he said, when he heard someone say "baby." He had stopped and listened, and when he heard her sobbing he crept up the steps. He did it only because he knew who the girl was. He was concerned about her. There was a family connection between the Rodriguezes and the Hawthornes, in the old days.

As Eduardo's message began to dawn, Carmelita sat down at the kitchen table. Waves of rage and nausea ebbed and flowed through her. The old man finished his tale. "Thank you," she said, and hung up. She sat a long time, her head bowed, cupped in her hands. She closed her eyes, but still the waves of red and green surged past them. She opened them. The bare lightbulb glared. Stars glinted around it. She realized that the stars were tears. She closed her eyes. She waited a long time, not thinking. Slowly, the red and green tides flowed away. She got up, leaning heavily on her palms, pressed against the tabletop. She raised her hands and looked at them, folded them into fists and raised them above her head.

"*Aaaaiiii!*" The walls of the kitchen seemed to vibrate. Rosa's door slammed, her bare feet slapped the linoleum, hurrying. Carmelita wheeled and pointed her finger.

"*Whore!*"

Rosa paled.

"Whore! The whore of Kevin Adams!"

"Mama!" Rosa rushed to her and tried to embrace her. Carmelita shoved her away. Rosa staggered backward against the refrigerator. Carmelita's eye fell on a butcher knife on the table. Two tiny bits of onion were stuck to the blade. She grabbed the knife.

"Mama!"

The word penetrated Carmelita's rage. She saw the knife in her hand and burst into tears. She hurled the knife to the floor. It skittered across the linoleum and banged against a chair. She fell to her knees and bent until her forehead touched the cold linoleum. Her noises wracked, as if she were a large animal wounded, trying to cough its blood. Rosa crumpled beside her and hugged her shoulders. "Mama."

Carmelita's voice was eerie, a ghost crying in the wind. *"I* am Kevin's whore."

"Mama."

"I bought you from him. He promised me."

"Mama, you don't know what you're saying!"

Carmelita didn't reply. Slowly she lifted her head and straightened her body until she was kneeling. Her voice was calm now. "You're pregnant?"

Rosa hesitated, then nodded slightly.

"Kevin is the father?"

"Yes!"

"And I am his whore."

"Mama, what do you mean?"

Carmelita got to her feet. "I've fucked him for months. He promised he would leave you alone if I fucked him. No. *I* offered to *fuck* him if he would leave you alone." She laughed bitterly. "I enjoyed it every time. I wasn't enough for him, eh?"

"I love him, Mama. I . . . It was *my* idea."

173

"And it was your idea to get pregnant?"

"No."

"Do you want to marry him?"

"Yes."

"Does he want to marry you?"

"Yes. I told him today. He needs time to think . . ."

"No time to *think!* He *will* marry you! I'm a crazy old *fool!* Don't go to school tomorrow. We have much to talk about, plans to make . . . Well, it's hard. Make some coffee. We'll be up late, eh?"

Rosa filled the pot and set it on the burner.

"How was he with you, Rosa? Was he gentle?"

Carmelita was sitting at the table now. Rosa glanced over her shoulder, but didn't reply until she had turned on the gas and sat down, too.

"Yes. It was lovely."

"Hmm!"

"Mama, never fuck him again!" Rosa's voice was brittle, challenging. "I *mean* it!"

Five

Kevin was surprised to feel the same sense of freedom that he had felt in other years on the last day of school before Christmas. His dreams the night before had been full of vague fears. He had awakened several times and had risen tired. But as the school day moved from half-hearted attempts at study in the morning to classroom parties, gift-givings and carol-singings in the afternoon, his body recovered its strength and recharged his mind. Now he drove toward Carmelita's house with Mary Beth's needlepoint chair cover gift-wrapped on the seat beside him. He sang "Joy to the World," loving the sound of his voice.

He wasn't the first to be in his situation. Tears would be shed. There would be gossip until the baby arrived. There would be counting to seven on fingers on the day of its birth, and hypocritical cooing when it was exhibited for the first time at the drugstore. Later, in the sewing-club and prayer-meeting circles, there would be clucks over the cute little couple who had made the best of a bad deal. That's the way it always was in Fort Appleby.

He would have to tell Mary Beth that he was going to father a Mexican, and was going to marry one. That would be hard. After all her tears were gone, she would try to reason with him, try to persuade him that he couldn't do what he was going to do. How would he support a wife and child? What about his plans for college? What about his glorious future? He didn't know the answers, but he knew that he would know them then. Something would happen. A way would open. He knew it.

He dreaded Carmelita more than his mother. He couldn't pretend he hadn't betrayed her. He couldn't tell her he hadn't done what he had promised he wouldn't do. Fort Appleby, and perhaps even Mary Beth, would regard him as confused, wrongheaded, and ungrateful. Mothers would fear him, and pray that his sin not be admired by their children. He would be a bookish, rebellious boy whose life had crashed on the rock of careless lust. He would be the example that proved the good sense of their prejudice. He could bear that. He knew it. But Carmelita. She was the cause of his fitful sleep and fearful dreams. He sang now, driving toward her house, because he had decided not to tell her. Not yet.

He parked and got out of the car. The northern sky above the peaks was dark purple. The stink of the oil wells beyond the mountains was upon the wind. The line of naked poplars along the side of Carmelita's yard swayed and hissed,

175

and Kevin hugged the package to his body to protect its red bow. He ran to the porch and knocked urgently at the door, shivering. Carmelita looked through the curtains, then turned the knob. He opened the screen and stepped inside and slammed the door.

"Brrr!" he said.

Carmelita was wearing a flowered apron and holding a small paring knife. She stepped forward and slashed with it, once. Pain stung at Kevin's left temple. He dropped the gift and grabbed at his head. Blood flowed against his hand. It ran down his wrist. "God!"

She watched him, her face dark and stony as an Indian's, her dark eyes glaring from the mask, the knife held loosely by thumb and finger in her open palm. Blood oozed between his fingers. She said, "Come to the kitchen." He followed her, dazed. "Sit down." She motioned toward the breakfast table with her knife. She opened a cupboard, took out a clean white dishtowel, shook out its folds and held it under the faucet. She wrung it and tossed it to Kevin. "Here. Hold this against it." He mopped at his face and looked at the towel, alarmed at how red it was. "Hold it against the cut!" she ordered. She rummaged in a drawer and found a roll of adhesive tape and got another towel and laid them on the table. "Put your head down there." She cut the hem of the towel with the knife, ripped it in two, and folded one half into a thick bandage. She ripped off strips of tape and stuck them in a row along the edge of the table, then took the wet towel from Kevin's hand and swabbed the wound. "You'll have a scar," she said.

"You could have killed me!"

"Yes. But it would have made me a lot of trouble, and would have made my grandchild fatherless, like my daughter."

Kevin tried to lift his head. She shoved it back to the table

176

and pressed the clean bandage against the wound. She reached for a strip of tape. "I was going to tell you," he said.

"So I did this, and now I won't get to see you squirm. Does it hurt? Eh?"

"A little. It throbs."

"It'll hurt more later."

She worked silently at the bandage. Kevin peered out the corners of his eyes, trying to glimpse her face, but she was standing behind him. At last he asked, "How badly have I hurt you?"

"You've broken my heart."

Kevin swallowed hard. "Carmelita . . ."

"What is it?"

"Tell me what I should say to you."

"Idiot, must I teach you everything? Tell me you love my daughter."

"I *do* love her."

"Like a sister?"

"No. Like a wife."

"You don't know what that means."

"I'll *learn* what it means."

"She'll *teach* you. Raise your head. Look at me."

He looked at her, and her eyes suddenly softened. "I've hated you for a whole day now," she said.

"I love you, Carmelita."

"How? Like a mother-in-law?"

"No."

"How, then?"

"I . . . I don't know."

"Like a woman, maybe?"

"Yes."

"Thank you for that, anyway. Of course, it must end."

"Yes."

177

"It would be sinful, making love to the grandmother of your child. And Rosa *would* kill you. How do you feel now?"

Kevin touched the bandage.

"Don't do that. You'll make the bleeding worse. I must call your mother."

"Why?"

"I'm taking you to Sharon and get that thing sewn up."

"She'll ask how it happened."

"I asked you to carry out the garbage, and, being clumsy, you fell against the gate."

"Where's Rosa? She wasn't at school."

"We talked about you all night. She's at the grocery now."

"Is she all right?"

"She'll live."

"I want her to go with us."

"No. You and I, we have a lot to talk about. Wash yourself."

Kevin unzipped his jacket and eased his bloody left hand through the sleeve. The sleeve was wet near the cuff. The blood had flowed down his arm and soaked his shirt. He moved to the sink and turned on the cold water, and plunged his arm, sleeve and all, under the icy stream. He listened to Carmelita lie to Mary Beth. As he watched the pink water turn clear again, swirling down the drain, she hung up. She untied her apron and laid it on the drainboard beside a bowl of potatoes. She fingered his bloody collar.

"You're a mess. These stains won't come out."

"It's okay. It's an old shirt."

"Take it off. I'll get you one."

She went into the bedroom and returned with a neatly ironed khaki shirt on a hanger. There were dark spots on the sleeves where Felipe's Army insignia had been. Kevin removed his shirt, laid it beside the apron, and took the clean one from the hanger.

"It swallows you," Carmelita said.

"Felipe was a big man."

"Yes. He was. Hurry. I want to leave before Rosa gets back."

They ran to the car. The wind was gusting through Victorio Canyon. The stink of the oil fields was stronger than before. "It's going to be very cold," she said.

"I hope it snows."

"You want a white Christmas, eh?"

"It would be different."

"This Christmas is different already."

The street was almost deserted. Lights burned in the few businesses that were still open. Carmelita's car was parked in front of the grocery store. She glanced toward the lighted plate-glass window. "Poor girl," she said. "How can she ever trust you?"

Kevin turned the car into the Sharon road and gunned it up the long hill. Then they wound toward the vast flat. Barely visible under the purple sky was another range of mountains, where Sharon nestled.

Six

It had snowed. Leaping Panther Mountain gleamed in sunlight. Its dazzling bulk was pocked with black, irregular forms of boulders and leafless oaks protruding through its white mantle. The locked-up cabins of the summer people and the narrow roads that sloped toward the larger houses of the town shared the mountain's veil of virginity. In the town, though, the streets already were tire-marked. Children shouted, popped their Christmas firecrackers, and

179

hurled snowballs at friends on shiny Christmas bicycles. It was the kind of Christmas Day that Fort Appleby always hoped for but seldom got, bright in snow and sunshine, cozy in fireplace aromas of burning oak and pine.

Kevin swept the snow from the windshield with his gloved hand. His face ached under its bandage. The engine was running. The old Ford had complained at first, coughing and sputtering out of its cold sleep, but now it rumbled contentedly.

Kevin stepped onto the running board and kicked the snow from his boots. He climbed in and turned the car into the street. In the plaza, a crowd of small Mexican boys bombarded the car with snowballs. Kevin waved and drove past the row of locked-up stores to Eisenbarger's house.

Eisenbarger greeted him in pajamas and robe.

"Merry Christmas," Kevin said.

"Merry Christmas. What happened to your face?"

"I fell against a gate."

"Was she pretty?"

"No. She was really a gate."

"Um."

The living room was strewn with wrapping paper and ribbon. Ginnie was playing with a red-haired doll under the tired-looking Christmas tree. "Kev!" she yelled. "Look!"

"Wow! Pretty!"

Genevieve lounged on the sofa. The frilly red hem of her nightgown peeked from the folds of her robe. She waved languidly. "Season's greetings and all that."

"Hi. You look tired."

"Midnight church services, playing S-a-n-t-a, a husband who won't let you sleep. It gets a body down."

Eisenbarger snickered. "We would offer you breakfast, but we just had it. How about some coffee?"

"Fine. I've already eaten, anyway."

Kevin followed Eisenbarger into the kitchen. "Mr. Jay," he said softly, "I know this is a bad time, but there's something I have to talk to you about."

Eisenbarger, pouring the coffee, glanced up. "What is it?"

"I hate to bring it up today. I don't want to disturb your Christmas."

Eisenbarger handed Kevin his cup. He frowned. "You want to talk in here, or go into the living room?"

"I'm going to be a father, Mr. Jay."

Eisenbarger turned to the stove. He shifted the pots and pans around on the burners, banging them busily. Then he said, "I see. That *is* serious. Well."

"I had to tell *some*body, Mr. Jay."

"Yes."

Genevieve appeared at the door, holding her empty cup. She saw the distress in Kevin's face. "What's the matter?"

Eisenbarger turned. He glanced at Kevin, then at Genevieve, then at Kevin again, questioning.

Kevin shrugged. "She might as well know. Everybody will know soon."

"What?" There was alarm in Genevieve's voice.

"Kevin tells me he's going to be a father."

Genevieve stared, stricken, at the boy. She set her cup on the table among the remains of the breakfast and hugged him. Her hair brushed his bandage. "Oh, Kevin."

"Come on, let's go to the living room," Eisenbarger said.

Ginnie, sitting in a small red wagon, was trying to pull the blue dress off of the doll. She glanced at them, then concentrated again on her task.

"Take off your coat, Kevin," Genevieve said. Then they sat in a row on the sofa, gazing at the child.

"Do you want to tell me who the girl is?" Eisenbarger asked.

181

"Rosa Hawthorne."

Eisenbarger nodded. "I see."

"Rosa's a nice girl," Genevieve said.

Silence descended. They sipped their coffee, watching Ginnie. She had tossed the doll under the Christmas tree and was throwing wooden blocks at it. She glanced at the trio on the sofa, surprised that they weren't objecting.

"Does your mother know?" Genevieve asked.

"Not yet."

"Does Rosa's mother know?"

"Yes."

"How does she feel about it?"

Kevin shrugged. "It's hard to tell."

Eisenbarger sighed. "Well, Kevin, what are you going to do?"

"Marry her, I guess. What else *can* I do?"

"You could deny paternity."

"Jay!"

Eisenbarger waved away Genevieve's objection. "He *could* do that."

"I couldn't," Kevin said.

"Well, you could run," Eisenbarger said.

"Where to?"

"Join the Army. Join the Navy and see the world. You can get your diploma in the service, you know."

"No, I'm going to marry her."

"How do you feel about her?"

"I love her."

"Really?"

"Yes."

"You're pretty young to know that. But, okay. Say you love her and you marry her. What do you do then?"

"I don't know."

"Are you going to stay in Fort Appleby?"

"Yes. Until I finish school, anyway."

"People aren't going to like that. They've spent half a century keeping the Anglos and the Mexicans apart. Officially, anyway."

"Jay!"

"It's okay," Kevin said. "So what will Fort Appleby do to us?"

"It'll hate you."

"Will it give me a job?"

"No. Not unless you become a Mexican. You won't be Anglo anymore. You'll be a Mexican. Do you want to be a Mexican?"

"I hadn't thought about it that way."

"Well, that's how it'll be." Eisenbarger set his cup on the coffee table. "Kevin, listen. You're graduating this year. You're going to be valedictorian. That gets you a year's tuition at any state college you want to go to. I could find you another scholarship somewhere, maybe even a job, if your mother can't support you. You've got a fine mind. You want to write books. You *can* write books if you try hard enough and long enough. But if you're going to start right off with a wife and kid . . . Jesus!"

"Mr. Jay, I already *have* a kid on the way! I'm going to *have* a wife!" He was shrill. His cheek throbbed. His head was beginning to ache. Ginnie shouted, "Kev! Shut up!" He waved at her. "I have to start from *there,*" he said quietly. *"Now* where do I go?"

"You stay in this town and you'll be another Emmy Hawthorne," Eisenbarger said. So will your child. Are you ready for that?"

"I don't know what that means."

"Neither do I, and I'll never find out. But *you* will, if you stay."

Genevieve's eyes narrowed. "Join the Army, Kevin.

183

Marry Rosa, and leave her here with her mother, and join the Army. Then come back and get your family and get out. Go to school on the GI Bill. You can have it *all*, Kevin. It'll take longer, but you can have it *all.*"

Ginnie picked up a terrycloth clown. She ran to Kevin and held it out to him. "Look!" she said. He took it from her and held it, studying its embroidered smile. He shook it, ringing the tiny bell at the tip of its cap, and handed it back to her. "Nice clown," he said. He stood up and reached for his coat. "I don't want to ruin your whole day."

Eisenbarger and Genevieve accompanied him to the front door. "Genevieve and I . . . We're your friends, Kevin," Eisenbarger said. "We'll help you any way we can."

"I know that."

"Wait." Eisenbarger walked to the bookcase and pulled out the little brown *Meditations* and laid it lovingly in Kevin's hands. "You should have it to keep."

"I . . . Thank you."

"Forget it."

Genevieve hugged Kevin. He kissed her on the cheek, then turned and embraced Eisenbarger. "That's what a Mexican would do," he said.

They stood on the porch while he walked to the car. He opened the door and called back to them, "Go inside. You'll freeze." But they stood there until he drove away.

Seven

He waited until the food was put away and the dinner dishes done, and then he told Mary Beth. Her eyes widened when he told her that Rosa was pregnant and that he was the father, but she said nothing. She rocked gently in the high-backed rocker by the fireplace while he spilled out his

184

love for Rosa, his intention to marry her, his confidence in the future, his dreams, his love for his mother, his anguish at hurting her, his desire to comfort her and protect her, his willingness to defy public opinion, his desire to hold on to his mother's love. It gushed from him like a flash flood while she rocked. Shock, confusion, anger, grief moved through her eyes while he spoke. Then, as suddenly as he had begun, he stopped. "Well . . ." he said, groping for another thought, another sentence, another word to fill the silence between them. But none came, and when the silence descended again, she burst into tears, and ran into her bedroom and slammed the door. He went to the door and called her. "Go away," she said. He went back to the living room and sat down, staring at the Christmas tree and its silly, candle-shaped lights that bubbled, and the small cluster of gifts, open and neatly displayed under the green boughs.

He sat for a long time, lighting one cigarette from another, not really thinking, just staring at the tree, wishing he was in another place, or that Jasper was with him, or that Rosa was with him, or that he was at the Four Leaf Clover Motel with that waitress from Castalon, or that he was drunk or dead. At last, he got up, his head foggy with tobacco and fatigue, aching, and walked into the yard. A million stars winked at him from the black sky. The moon, full and silver, cast a blue glow over the snow. A small dog at some house near the foot of Leaping Panther yapped shrilly. The animal's silly excitement and a slight breeze through the leafless branches of the trees were the only sounds in the town. Kevin sniffed the cold air, welcoming the surge of fresh blood it sent to his brain, and squinted toward the mountain. As his eyes adjusted to the darkness, he could make out the ridge line. In his mind, he walked over Leaping Panther's windy crest, remembering the stunted oak under which he so often rested, a distinctive boulder here, a giant yucca there, the rustle of wind through the long, dry grass, a jackrabbit scurrying and then stopping stone-still, believing himself to be invisible. He had never seen it at night or in the snow, and he toyed with the thought of going there now. But he knew he couldn't find his footholds at night, in the snow, even with a light, and he would fall and be broken, and would die before he was found.

He had been in bed a long time, but hadn't slept, when Mary Beth came into his room. "Kevin," she said into the darkness.

"Yes?"

"Are you awake?"

"Yes."

"I want you to leave."

Kevin frowned, straining to see her face. He couldn't. "What?"

"I want you to leave this house, Meskin-lover. Tonight. Now." Her voice was calm, almost gentle. She didn't come near the bed.

"Mother . . ."

"Now. Get dressed and get out."

"Where can I go?"

"I don't know. I don't care. Go to your Meskin whore. Don't come back, Kevin. I'll send your things wherever you want."

"Mother . . ."

"Don't be here in the morning."

Her robe rustled, and the door closed softly. Kevin lay back, confused, angry, afraid. Slowly the anger overcame the fear and confusion, and he got up and turned on the light. He dressed, deliberately choosing his warmest cloth-

186

ing, stuffing his coat pockets with socks and underwear. He pulled his gray whipcord suit out of the closet and slung it over his shoulder. He stepped into the night and zipped his coat and strode to Jasper's car.

The plastic seatcovers were cold and brittle. The steering gear, stiff with cold, responded slowly to his hands. He drifted slowly down the street, as he had after hearing the news of Jasper, keeping the car in ruts that other cars had left in the snow. He drifted by San Ignacio Church, down the long hill, past Old Fort Appleby. He started to turn toward Carmelita's, but no lights were burning. He glanced at his watch. It was almost one o'clock. The heater was beginning to warm the car now. "Think," he told himself. "You've got to think. This is serious." His brain responded only with jumbled images of his mother, the fireplace, the Christmas tree, wraiths of snow moving across the highway on the wind. Like an old horse going home, independent of its rider's will, the car moved up Victorio Canyon, its tires spinning on the slick hills. The rattle of the cattleguard was brittle, musical, in the cold. The tires slid on the round creek rocks. Kevin wrestled the steering wheel, took control. He was going somewhere now. He followed deep tire tracks up the narrow road, around the tight curves. The ranch buildings were dark. He pulled up at the gate of the headquarters house and cut the engine and the lights. He walked through untracked snow up the path and the steps and opened the door.

The cold inside was old and still, deeper than the wind outside. He found the light switch beside the door and flipped it, bathing the room in yellow light. He rubbed his hands together. He was very cold. He glanced toward the creek-rock fireplace and was grateful that four oak logs were in the black iron wash pot beside it. A newspaper lay on the gaudily striped serape that covered the sofa. He picked it up and read the date, August 31, and crumpled it sheet by sheet and laid the wads in the grate. He arranged three of the logs on the paper and struck a match, his hand red, shivering.

The logs were beginning to catch when the door opened. Jimmy George Duncan held a revolver. His arm was down, not threatening, the gun's muzzle pointed toward the floor. "Kevin!" he said. "I figured it was you, soon as I saw the car. What the hell you doing?"

"Trying to get warm, right now."

The foreman closed the door. "What you doing here, son?"

The logs were going to burn. Kevin stood up, his back to the fire. "You mind if I sleep here? I would have asked you first, but I figured you were asleep."

"Yeah, son. It's all right. But what you doing out here?"

"Mother kicked me out. I couldn't think of anyplace else to go."

"Oh. Pretty bad, huh?"

"Yeah."

"What happened to your face?"

"Accident."

Jimmy George laid the revolver on the mantel and stood beside Kevin, warming his hands. "Helluva night to be out wandering around." He started to unbutton his coat, then noticed the one log remaining in the wash pot. "I'll get some more firewood," he said.

"No. Don't bother . . ."

"You're going to need it. It's colder than an Eskimo's balls out there." He tugged at his hatbrim and walked outside.

The fire was taking the chill off the small room. Kevin pulled a heavy, rawhide-seated chair close to the fireplace and sat down, holding his palms out to the fire. Then Jimmy

George kicked at the door, and Kevin rose and opened it. The foreman's face was hidden behind his load. He carried the logs to the wash pot and dropped them with a bang and pushed his hat to the back of his head.

"Celebrated Christmas yet?" he asked cheerily.

"Yeah. Up to a point."

"I haven't." He pulled a pint bottle of bourbon out of his coat pocket and held it up. "Join me?"

"Sure. I could use one."

"Figured you could." He took off his hat and coat and tossed them on the sofa. He pulled up another rawhide chair beside Kevin's and sat down. "You don't mind it straight out of the bottle, do you?"

"No."

"Some folks don't like to drink after others."

"I don't mind." Kevin took off his coat and tossed it on the sofa, too, and resumed his seat.

Jimmy George popped up. "Let's make it *look* Christmasy," he said. He turned off the light. The room became a dark cave, the flames casting dancing, mysterious shadows on the ceiling and walls. "Better, ain't it?"

"Yeah."

Jimmy George sat down and uncorked the bottle and offered it to Kevin. "Well, merry Christmas," he said.

The liquor burned Kevin's throat and hit his stomach like a hot coal. He coughed and handed the bottle back. "Merry Christmas," he rasped.

"Too strong for you? I'll get some water . . ."

"No. I'll get used to it. Feels good."

"Sure warms you up, don't it?" Jimmy George drank from the bottle and held it in his lap. The flames cast shadows in the deep wrinkles and crevices of his face and neck. "I sure like fireplaces," he said. "I wish my house had one."

"Yeah. They're nice." Kevin held out his hand, and Jimmy George gave him the bottle. The whiskey went down more smoothly this time.

"We had a fireplace when we was up on the UP, where I growed up. You know the UP? Presidio County. Down by the river."

"I've heard of it. Never been there."

"Ain't worth a shit. My daddy worked there all his life. I left and come up here when I was just a tad. I like the Circle-B. Fine place."

Kevin took another swig before he handed the bottle back to Jimmy George. The whiskey was getting to him, making him feel good. "You want to know why my old lady kicked me out?"

"I wasn't going to ask."

"I knocked up a girl."

"No shit!"

"You want to know who it is? Rosa Hawthorne."

"Gregorio's granddaughter?"

"I'm going to marry her."

"No shit." Jimmy George gazed into the fire. "You know, that happened to me once. At least I *think* it did. Me and Carl went down to Del Rio once to buy some cows, and I met this waitress. Mildred was her name. Well, I tumbled her, and a couple months later I get this letter from her, saying she's knocked up and wants to marry me."

"What did you do?"

"Nothing. I didn't answer the letter."

"You got a kid running around out there somewhere."

"He'd be growed up by now. That was way long years ago. If that bitch wasn't lying."

"You wonder about it?"

"Sometimes."

"Maybe you should have married her."

"Nope. Some folks was meant for marrying, but I ain't."

Kevin took another swallow of whiskey. His nose and fingertips were tingling. His lips were numb. "Well, I'm going to marry Rosa."

"Don't blame you. Cute girl."

"She's a Mexican."

"Don't matter. They're all made alike."

"It's nice of you to let me stay here, Jimmy George."

"Hell, I'm glad to have you. I don't think Carl would mind. Glad to have you around. I ain't seen a white man in over a week."

"I'm liable to stay for some time."

"Fine. You can eat with me."

Kevin studied the crevices of the foreman's face. "Jimmy George," he said, "what's the most important thing that ever happened to you?"

He raised his bushy eyebrows. "Most important? Let me think." He gazed into the fire a moment, then grinned and crossed his legs. "I tracked a bear up the north slope of Star Mountain once. Found him, too. Shot him. Turned out to be the biggest bear ever killed in Davis County. The governor came to town not long after that, campaigning, I guess. Governor Beauford Jester. Fine man. Carl served him a bear steak and gave him that bear hide as a souvenir. He let me present it to him. I guess that's the most important thing I ever done. Way long years ago."

"That's something. The governor, huh?"

"Yeah. Governor Beauford Jester."

"That's something. It sure is."

When Kevin passed out, Jimmy George picked him up and laid him on the sofa. He folded the serape over him and put two more logs on the fire and went home.

The aromas of bacon and coffee awakened him. Jimmy George set the plate and the cup on the coffee table. Kevin sat up.

"How you feeling, son?"

"My head's about to bust."

"Eat and feel better."

Kevin wolfed the thick-sliced bacon and scrambled eggs and biscuits. Jimmy George sat and watched him, rolling cigarettes with his stubby, calloused fingers, smoking. "I was figuring on riding out, seeing if any cows got caught in the drifts. It's a pretty day. Maybe you'd like to come along."

"Sure."

"Fine. I'll go saddle up."

Kevin rode the pinto that Emiliano was sitting on in the picture at the dance. He was a tough, stocky little animal, frisky, snorting in the cold air. The day was bright. Everything looked new.

Mary Beth met Carmelita at the door. "You don't work here anymore," she said.

"Let me come inside. Let's talk."

Mary Beth hesitated, then stood aside. Carmelita took off her coat. "I know how you feel," she said. "I've been wronged, too."

"She's your daughter."

"He's your son."

They glared at each other. Then Carmelita's eyes softened, became contrite. "I lost control, like you. I'm a widow, Mrs. Adams, like you. I need the work."

Mary Beth didn't answer.

"The house is a mess, Mrs. Adams, and I need the work. Please."

Mary Beth looked at her watch. "All right," she said. "Start in Kevin's room. Change the sheets."

Eight

The wind was whipping the poplars, but Rosa was waiting with her suitcase on the front porch, her coat collar pulled up around her face. She ran to the car and got in, shivering.

"God, if I'd been late, you would have frozen," Kevin said.

"I was praying you would get here before Mama did. There would have been a scene."

"She wants me to marry you."

"Yes, but she wants it in the church."

"It's better this way. Leaving everyone out of it but us."

"I hope this jalopy makes it."

"Learn to love it, honey. It's the only car we've got."

She took off her long green coat and tossed it into the back seat, then snuggled against him. Her short red curls were cool against his cheek.

"Black!" he said. "You're wearing black to your wedding?"

She wore a black faille sheath, sleeveless, with a rhinestone pin on her left shoulder. "It's my best dress. Don't you like it?"

"Yes, but isn't black bad luck for weddings? Isn't that why they wear white?"

She smiled. "White is for virgins. I don't qualify, thanks to you. Bridegrooms are supposed to wear black, which you're not."

Kevin was wearing the old gray whipcord western suit

193

and his maroon boots. "I feel like we're on a date," he said. "My first date with you."

"From now on, all your dates will be with your wife . . . That's a scary word, wife."

"Are you scared?"

"This is a scary thing we're doing, isn't it? Aren't *you* scared?"

"A little. Nervous, anyway."

"Me, too."

"Do you love me?" he asked. "Do you really want to marry me?"

"Yes, Mr. Adams. I love you, and I want to marry you."

"I love you."

"I believe you."

He patted her belly. "How's what's-his-name?"

"Barely there. No trouble at all."

"Hardly enough to get married over."

"He'll get bigger. I've got to catch you before I get fat and ugly."

It was eighty miles to the border. They drove through Presidio and crossed the rickety bridge at dusk, into the rag-tag collection of low adobe buildings that is Ojinaga. Bits of paper danced along the sidewalks in the cold wind. The benches around the plaza were empty. Sand stood in small drifts along the curbs. The curio shops were closed. Sad *mariachi* music drifted from behind the closed door of a bar, a trumpet wailing mournfully among guitars.

"Where do we go?" Kevin asked.

"Drive around the plaza. Look for a sign."

"Saying what?"

"I don't know."

The old Ford crept along the narrow street. Kevin and Rosa squinted at the dirty, cracked stucco fronts of the buildings, in the failing light, searching for some sign of

194

judicial authority. Rosa pointed. "Up there, I think."

A small, dim lightbulb swayed above a sign, so weathered it was almost illegible.

MATRIMONIO
DIVORCIO

The forefinger of a peeling gilt hand slanted under the peeling gilt letters, pointed accusingly at a small closed door.

"One-stop shopping," Kevin said. He parked the car under the sign, and Rosa put on her coat. They got out and tried the door. It was locked. A bell cord hung beside the door. Rosa pulled it. The door opened almost immediately, and an old woman, her head wrapped in a black shawl, peered out. Rosa spoke to her in Spanish. The woman nodded and opened the door. She directed them up dark, narrow stairs. Rough adobe bricks glared through large holes in the dingy white plaster of the walls. At the landing, the woman parted a tattered red-velvet curtain and motioned for them to enter. Except for a small desk and a Mexican flag draped on the wall behind it, and two old-fashioned round-backed chairs, the room was empty. It smelled of dust. The old woman opened another door and disappeared, leaving it ajar. A child cried out somewhere in the recesses of the building.

Kevin took Rosa's hand. "Are you sure this is the place?"

"Yes."

The door opened. A dark, fat man emerged, smiling, his teeth as white as his rumpled shirt. His bald scalp reflected the light of the yellow bulb hanging from the twisted cord in the center of the ceiling. He rubbed his hands together. "You wish to be married?" His huge black mustache moved as he spoke.

"Yes," Kevin said.

"You have ten dollars?"

"Yes."

The man nodded. "That is what it costs." He sat down at the desk, opened a drawer, and pulled out a pad. He dipped an old-fashioned pen into an inkwell and scratched on the pad. "The thirty-first of December, nineteen hundred and fifty-two," he said. "You will be my last wedding this year, I think. The bridegroom's name?"

"James Kevin Adams."

"Age?"

"Seventeen."

"Place of residence?"

"Fort Appleby, Texas."

"The bride's name?"

"Rosalinda Hawthorne," Rosa said. "H-a-w-t-h-o-r-n-e."

"Age?"

"Eighteen."

"Place of residence?"

"The same as his."

The man wrote, then grunted and laid down the pen. He pulled a small book from the drawer and stood up. He held out his palm. "May I have the ten dollars, please?" Kevin gave him the money, and the man called, "Maria! Hector!" A dumpy, middle-aged woman and a young, fat, curly-haired man came through the door and stood beside the desk. They were chewing. The woman smacked her lips.

The man read rapidly in Spanish from the book. Whenever he looked at Rosa, Rosa said, "I do." Whenever he looked at Kevin, Kevin said, "I do." It was done in two minutes. The man said, "Kiss the bride." Kevin pecked Rosa on the lips, the witnesses signed the paper, and the man tore it off the pad and handed it to Kevin. "Your receipt," he said.

"Receipt?"

"Your marriage certificate." He grinned his pearly grin and shook Kevin's hand. "Congratulations, and happy New Year." He pulled back the velvet curtain and pointed down the stairs. "That is the way out."

On the sidewalk, Kevin took Rosa in his arms. "Now I want to *really* kiss the bride," he said. He kissed her slowly, gently.

"Oh, Kevin, it was *awful*, wasn't it?"

"It doesn't matter. We're married. That's what counts, isn't it, Mrs. Adams?"

"Yes, that's what counts."

He kissed her forehead. "You're beautiful, Mrs. Adams. How about a drink to celebrate?"

She glanced across the plaza at the dingy windows of the bar where the *mariachis* blared. "I don't want to go in there."

"Wait in the car, then. I'll see if I can get something to go."

He trotted across the plaza and returned in a few minutes carrying two paper cups. He clutched a brown paper bag under his arm. Rosa opened the door and took the drinks. He laid the bag in the back seat. "A pint of bourbon for us and a fifth of tequila for Jimmy George," he said.

Rosa handed him a cup, and he raised it in a toast. "To my lovely bride."

"To my lovely husband. And a happy new year."

A fire blazed in the fireplace. A new fifth of bourbon anchored a note to the mantel.

"Dear Kevin & Rosa, I dont have no shampane, but this stuff is pretty good. I laid a fire in the stove in Carls room & changed the sheets. Its the best room in the house & I

197

dont think he wuld mind. Congrats and happy new year. Your frend, JGD."

"Old Jimmy George," Kevin said. "I bet it took him all day to write this."

"Pour us a drink," Rosa said. "I'll put on something sexy and make you very excited, and you will be extremely passionate all night long." She kissed the tip of his nose and picked up her suitcase and walked into the dark, cold hallway.

JANUARY, 1953

JANUARY 1978

One

Of course, they were the talk of the school. Mexican girls gathered around Rosa in the hallway, exclaiming over the plain gold band that Kevin had placed on her hand in front of the fireplace. He had forgotten it until he took off his coat and touched it in the pocket. The girls whispered questions. Rosa answered behind her hand, and the girls giggled. Rosa enjoyed it.

But Kevin was shut out. Julio Garcia and other Mexican boys who had liked him nodded curtly when he spoke, but wouldn't look him in the eye. The Anglo boys, who customarily gathered in tight groups around the radiators in the classrooms until the teacher ordered them to sit down, cut off their talk and drifted toward their desks when Kevin entered a room. Anglo girls, sweatered and ponytailed, stared during class. A mixture of curiosity and resentment burned in their eyes whenever he caught them. Then they would turn away. His teachers, who usually turned to him when no one else would answer a question, didn't call on him. Whenever Kevin addressed them, they replied in tight-lipped monosyllables. Only Eisenbarger pretended that nothing had changed. He lectured enthusiastically about "Wild Bill" and Macbeth as if the rules of life were still intact, and the ring on Rosa's finger didn't exist, and the bright red scar on Kevin's cheek was the only change in the universe. Kevin loved him during that hour, and wished that he could walk up the aisle and embrace him as he had on Christmas Day.

At the end of the period, Kevin waited behind Alicia

Jones for his turn at the water fountain. She drank and wiped her mouth with the back of her hand. Then she smiled. "Well, hi, stud."

"Hi, Alicia."

"Exciting holidays, weren't they?" She touched the scar. "Souvenir of the honeymoon?"·

"An accident."

"My. Accidents are happening to you all over the place, aren't they?" Her smile softened. "I knew, didn't I?"

"Yeah."

"Well, don't let them get you down."

"Who?"

"You know. Them. Everybody. They'll get over it."

"I wish I believed that."

"They will." She touched the scar again. "Real sexy." She wrinkled her nose and tripped away.

He stepped into the restroom. Clay Sanger was wetting his comb under the faucet, slicking his hair back from his square face. Kevin walked behind him to the urinal. Clay glanced at him in the mirror and sniffed. *"Whew!* I smell a Meskin in here!" Kevin didn't reply. Clay took care, arranging his long hair behind his ears. "I wonder how it feels to be a greaser," he said to his image in the glass. "I hear greasers are good ass. I didn't think a white man had to *become* one to find out, though. Sure didn't. Why, you can *hire* one in Ojinaga for just . . ."

Kevin buttoned his fly, then pivoted quickly. The suddenness of the move alerted Clay. He turned and crouched, grinning. "Awright, come on, Adams. Come and get it. I'm going to whip your chili-loving ass."

Kevin took one long step, and swung his leg fast and hard, as if kicking a football. The sharp toe of his boot slammed into Clay's groin. Clay's face contorted. He went pale and collapsed onto the stone floor. Kevin leaped upon

202

him and straddled him. He dug frantically into his pocket and pulled his knife and opened the smallest blade and moved it slowly toward Clay's gasping, crying face. "Don't move around so much, Sanger," he said quietly. "If it slips, I'll get your throat." Clay screamed as the sharp blade cut into his ear. Kevin neatly sliced off the lobe. He grabbed Clay's outstretched hand and placed the bit of flesh in the palm and closed the fingers over it. "Next time, this is your balls." Through the haze of his anger he saw two small boys standing, wide-eyed, and heard voices at the door. Then Eisenbarger was there, his paddle dangling from his wrist as he held a paper towel under the still-flowing faucet and slapped it onto Clay's bleeding head.

"Get up, Adams!" he yelled over Clay's screams. "Get the hell up! Go to my office and stay there!"

Kevin got up and dragged himself wearily out the door. His stomach churned. His heart beat furiously. He flopped into the chair beside Eisenbarger's desk and held his head in his hands, barely aware of the chatter of children, a woman's shrill questions, Eisenbarger barking orders. He watched without interest as Eisenbarger struggled past the door, trying to hold Clay's heavy body erect. Children followed them in a cluster. They stared at Kevin, whispering, then ran past. Slowly the building stilled. Only the pompous tick of the clock intruded into Kevin's anger and remorse and fear.

Eisenbarger returned and slumped into his swivel chair. They gazed sadly at one another. "Well, is this the way you're going to handle it?" Eisenbarger asked quietly. Kevin didn't answer. Eisenbarger asked again, insistently, "*Is* it?"

"Mr. Jay, he . . ."

Eisenbarger raised his hand. "I don't want to hear it. Is this the way you're going to *handle* it?"

203

Kevin shrugged. "I'm sorry. He made me so mad, I . . ."

"You're a savage, Kevin," Eisenbarger said softly.

"I didn't kill him. I could have. I wanted to."

"You just mutilated him. How humane!"

"How is he?"

"He'll be all right. So long as he doesn't want to wear earrings." Eisenbarger smiled wanly, then took off his glasses and rubbed his eyes. "You'll be in trouble if he goes to the law."

"He won't."

"No, I guess he won't. Your behavior just isn't that abnormal in Fort Appleby, unfortunately. Sometimes I think that in a hundred years this town hasn't learned a damn thing about decency. It's got a courthouse, it's got churches, it's got schools, but they don't make any difference. If things get tough, somebody goes for a gun or a knife or tries to gnaw a hole in somebody's throat. Or they just stand around and snicker at other people's troubles. I expected better of you, though. Would you really castrate him?"

"No. I was just trying to scare him."

"Well, you did. Are your troubles over now?"

"No."

"No, I don't think they are. What you need more than anything else right now, Kevin, is friends. Regardless of how you must be feeling now, you still have some. If I were you, I would try to hang on to them."

"Turn the other cheek, in other words."

"Yes, damn it, if that's what it takes!"

"And then what?"

"Endure. Or leave."

Eisenbarger lit a cigarette and blew the smoke toward the clock. "Well, Kevin, I've got to do *something*. I'm going to suspend you for two weeks. I hope people will consider that punishment enough. I would hate for them to think I'm going easy on you. I hope Clay's parents don't file charges. I hope it'll give people enough time to cool off. I hope you'll do some hard thinking, and straighten out your life." He rolled his chair away from the desk and stood up. Kevin stood up, too, and was ashamed of the tears he saw in Eisenbarger's eyes. "You can still make something of yourself, Kevin. Please don't mess it up."

Kevin walked quickly through the empty hall and out the back door. Rosa was waiting for him in the car at the front of the school, but he wanted to flee, to rest, to be alone. He walked toward the football field. He slowed his pace when he reached the frozen earth of the running track. He crammed his hands deep into his pockets and gazed about him at the expanse of brown, brittle grass and, beyond the fence, the bare, reaching branches of the elms and cotton-woods in the yards and vacant lots of the town. They looked like withered arms praying or despairing. Over the roof-tops, Leaping Panther Mountain loomed almost black under the gloomy sky. It wasn't a heartening sight. When Rosa saw him and honked the horn, he was ready to run to the car.

"What were you doing out there?" she asked.

"Just thinking."

"Are you staying for basketball practice?"

"No. I'm not playing anymore. I have more important things to think about now."

"Where's your coat?" she asked.

TWO

Elmer Martin sat on one of his fountain stools, hunched over the counter. He shook his head and sipped his coffee again. "You know how slow things are till the summer people get here," he said. "They might not even *come* this year. Fort Appleby's just another little Texas town now. It gets polio, too."

"You know *anybody* who's looking for help?"

"Naw, Kevin, I don't. If I hear of anything, I'll let you know."

"Thanks."

"Hey, want some coffee? I'll buy. A wedding present."

"Thanks. I might as well."

Martin climbed down from the stool and walked around the counter. "Naw, this is sure a bad time to be looking for a job." He tipped the steaming glass pot over the cup. "You need cream?"

"No."

"This time of year, me and my wife are really more people than we need in this place. If this was a hundred years ago, you know what I'd do? Hitch up a wagon and head west. Free land and opportunity. A man didn't have to go around looking for a job in those days, or sit on his ass waiting for the summer people to come."

"Yeah, but those days are long gone."

"Yeah. Unless you go up to Alaska. I hear they still homestead up there."

"Too far. And too cold."

"Yeah. I don't see how them Eskimos stand it. I can barely stand *Texas* in the winter. I'd like to be in Florida right now. Or Hawaii. Or Acapulco. Some place warm.

206

Hey, how would you like to buy this place?"

"I don't have the money."

"Could you get it? I'd let you have it cheap."

"No, I don't think I could get it."

"Oh. Well, you wouldn't like it anyway. It's awful confining. Especially on days like today. Nobody comes in. I get lonesome. Hey, why ain't you in school today?"

"I got suspended yesterday."

"Oh, yeah. I heard you had some trouble."

"Yeah."

"Not serious, I hope."

"No."

"Hey, what do you think of Callahan resigning? That was a surprise, wasn't it?"

"I hadn't heard."

"Yeah, he's getting out of the preaching business. He got hisself a job as radio dispatcher, somewhere around Odessa, I think. I don't blame him. She's a beautiful woman. And I guess it wouldn't do, a preacher keeping company with a woman that ain't even divorced yet."

"I guess not."

"A man's got to do what he's got to do, right?"

"Right."

"I don't hold it against you."

"What?"

"Well, you know how people feel . . . I just wanted you to know I don't hold it against you."

"Oh. Well, I'd better go. Thanks for the coffee."

"Don't mention it. I'd tell you to ask around some of the ranches, but they usually don't hire men in the winter, either."

"Yeah. Well, if you hear of something, let me know."

"Sure. A radio dispatcher. I bet he'll like that. I wouldn't mind doing that myself."

"Yeah, he'll probably like it."

"You know, one thing I've been wondering about. If God calls a man to be a preacher, how does he figure out that God doesn't want him to be a preacher anymore?"

"Maybe he just decides God was wrong."

Martin laughed. "That would take some guts, wouldn't it?"

"Yeah. Or maybe a beautiful woman."

Martin laughed and slapped the counter. "Oh, my! Oh, my, that *is* a good one! I'll remember that one! I sure will!"

Three

He was lying face down in the corral, a bridle clutched in his hand. The snow was flurrying. Thin, lacy flakes powdered his sandy hair and the fleece of his coat collar. The big roan snuffled him. The steam from his nostrils blew snowflakes off the leather coat.

Kevin waved his arms. "Get away, boy! Get out!" The horse pivoted on his hind legs and trotted across the corral. He nickered and nuzzled the pinto, standing, head down, against the rail fence. Kevin turned the body over and laid his cold palm against the wrinkled cheek. Jimmy George was still warm, but he was dead. Kevin jerked his hand away. He climbed over the fence and ran to the headquarters house. "Rosa!"

She appeared at the door, hugging herself in the cold.

"Jimmy George is dead!"

"Oh, my God!"

"In the corral! He's dead, Rosa!"

They went inside and stood in front of the fireplace. Kevin stared into the flames, concentrating, trying to slow the whirl of his mind.

"What can we *do?*" Rosa wrung her hands.

"Go to his house. See if he has a phone number for the Birdsongs. I'll try to bring him in."

Rosa put on her coat, and they walked together to Jimmy George's little house. "I don't want to go in," she said.

"Go in. It's all right."

Kevin returned to the corral and swung open the gate, careful to stay between the gate and the horses. He grabbed Jimmy George under the arms and lifted. He was heavier than he looked. Kevin tried to stand him upright, then stooped and grabbed him around the knees and heaved him onto his shoulder. He staggered, then recovered his balance and walked to the house.

The bed had been made, neat under a heavy black-and-white Mexican blanket. Kevin dropped Jimmy George to the blanket. Rosa, in the kitchen, glanced in, then away. "I think the number's here. It says, 'Gonzales.' "

"Yes, that will be it." Kevin arranged Jimmy George's arms straight along his sides, then went to the kitchen and cranked the phone.

"Number, please," Amy Ferguson said.

"Long distance. Person-to-person for Carl Birdsong." He read her the number, scrawled in pencil on the stuccoed wall.

"Who *is* this?"

"Kevin Adams."

"Oh. You."

"I'm in a hurry, Amy. Please get me that number."
Birdsong answered.

"Mr. Birdsong? Kevin Adams."

"Kevin! How are you?"

"Mr. Birdsong, Jimmy George is dead."

"Dead? What? Jimmy George?"

"Yes, sir."

209

There was a long pause, then, "What happened?"

"I don't know, sir. Heart attack, I guess. I found him in the corral."

There was another pause. "Have you made any . . . arrangements?"

"No, sir. I just found him. I brought him to the house. That's all."

"It's too bad. He was a good man. Listen. Call the funeral home at Sharon and have them pick him up. There's a plane to El Paso. It gets there about nine o'clock, I think. Can you meet me?"

"Yes, sir."

"Bring Vera's Cadillac. It's fast and comfortable."

"All right, sir."

"Kevin. I appreciate it. Jimmy George told me you were out there."

"I figured he had."

"Is everything all right . . . otherwise?"

"Yes, sir. Fine."

"Meet me at nine o'clock. In the Cadillac. Okay?"

"Yes, sir."

"Hey, wait a minute. Here's somebody that wants to talk to you."

There was silence, then a husky growl. "How's the old married man?"

"Jasper! Son of a bitch! How the hell you doing?"

"Fine. Swimming a lot."

"Swimming?"

"Yeah."

"Lucky bastard. It's colder than an Eskimo's balls here."

"I'll be there before long."

"Really? When?"

"Couple of months, maybe."

"Buddy, that's great! We'll have a helluva time!"

"Well, I just wanted to tell you congratulations."

"Thanks."

"Here's Daddy again."

"Kevin, fill up the Cadillac before you leave. At the Gulf station. Charge it to me."

Kevin stayed with Rosa until the funeral-home people took Jimmy George away, but he arrived in El Paso by seven o'clock. He decided to kill the two hours downtown. He parked the Cadillac in a lot and ate a chicken-fried steak and French fries at the Mills Restaurant, then walked down the block to San Jacinto Plaza. Although the evening was chilly, the plaza was busy. Soldiers wandered in pairs, turning to stare at the backsides of young Mexican mothers herding children toward the orange buses on Mills Street. Old Mexican maids in black shawls and darned cotton stockings waited on the benches, hugging brown shopping bags, chattering in high, whinny squawks. On the Mesa Street side, a red-faced, blue-suited evangelist railed at a small knot of listeners, his eyes frantic and rolling, his fist pounding the open Bible in his palm. Kevin wandered to the pond in the center of the plaza and peered into the murky water, trying to find the alligators. A drunk leaned on the rail beside him. The neck of a small bottle protruded from the pocket of his ragged suitcoat. He squinted at Kevin in the darkness. "They ain't there," he said. "They store them somewheres in the winter."

"Oh."

"You from out of town?"

"Yes."

"Well, you couldn't know, then."

Kevin nodded and turned away.

"Hey, buddy," the drunk said, "could you spare a nickel for a cup of coffee?"

Kevin fished in his pocket and handed him a quarter.

"Thanks, buddy." The man sighed. "Oh, Lordy, I wisht I was someplace else."

"Where?"

"La Tuna Federal Correctional Institution, that's where."

"Jail?"

The man snorted. "More like a hotel. No bars. Warm. The food's good, too." He paused, then whined, "Trouble is, you have to break a federal law to get in there, and I don't know which ones is federal. With my luck, I'd wind up in the City Jail with drunks puking on me."

"That wouldn't be any good."

"Naw, I can't take a chance on that."

"Well, enjoy your coffee."

"Thanks, buddy."

Kevin walked to the parking lot and tipped the attendant a quarter. He turned the car into Mills, then into Mesa and toward the Texas Western campus. He drove slowly past the buildings of the college, squinting at their strange, dark bulk. Texas Western looked like no college he had seen in pictures. No red bricks and ivy. He thought the architecture must be Spanish. Moorish, maybe. Lights burned in nearly all the buildings, and what he could see of their interiors looked cozily academic. Two coeds, walking toward the library with books clutched to their breasts, waved at him. He honked the horn and smiled, wondering whether they thought they knew him, or just wanted to get to know the Cadillac. He wished he was walking with them, with books clutched to his breast.

He turned the Cadillac around the brown grassy triangle and toward the airport. He lost his way among one-way streets and had to stop at a gas station to ask directions. Carl Birdsong's big silver plane, its propellers churning, was taxiing in by the time he reached the gate. Birdsong walked down the stairs carefully, holding his gray Stetson on his head with one hand and grasping the handrail with the other. He smiled wanly when he saw Kevin and strode over, his hand outstretched.

"How are you, son? It's good to see you."

"Fine. How are you?"

"I'm whipped. I hate those damn planes. Let's get a cup of coffee."

They sat on small round stools at the snack counter, Birdsong shifting uncomfortably. "There's nothing I hate worse than a chair without a back," he said. "Even a saddle had a little bit of back on it."

Kevin smiled. "It's good to see you again, sir."

"It's good to be back. It's been a long time, hasn't it?"

"How's Jasper doing?"

Birdsong's dark eyes lit up. "He's doing fine! Just fine! Those physical therapy people down there know their stuff. It's slow, though."

"He told me he's coming home soon."

"Yeah. Pretty soon, I guess. But it won't be the same, Kevin. I don't guess it'll ever be the same. He'll be in a wheelchair. And then on crutches. There'll always be braces, I guess. Jasper's got a lot of adjustments to make with his life." He set down his cup. "Well, let's head out."

Kevin stashed Birdsong's suitcase in the trunk of the Cadillac and unlocked the door. He was surprised at the man's awkwardness as he got into the car. He moved slowly, deliberately, like an old man. Birdsong sighed as he leaned into the Cadillac's plush cushions. "Oh, blessed-ness!" he said. "This beats the hell out of that plane."

Kevin urged the car swiftly through the suburban traffic to U.S. 80 and turned eastward. Birdsong, his Stetson set squarely on his head, looked around him as if he had never seen the lights of the little farm villages before. They stopped at a traffic light in Fabens, and Birdsong drank in the bleak surroundings. Weathered storefronts, Mexicans in overalls, battered pickups, a brown cur walking sideways to the wind. "Three hundred years ago, the Spaniards called this *El Camino Real,*" he said. "The Royal Highway. Nothing royal about it now, is there? It's just another road. Going God-knows-where."

The light changed, and Kevin touched the accelerator, thrilling at the car's almost silent burst of power.

"Changes and adjustments," Birdsong muttered. "Changes and adjustments."

"What?"

"Nothing. Just talking to myself. Feeling sorry for myself, I guess."

They didn't speak again until the Cadillac cleared the town and sped into the open country. Then Birdsong said, "There's been some changes in your life, too."

"Yeah."

"How do you feel about it?"

"I'm not used to it yet, but I'm not unhappy about it."

"Uh-huh. And how are things at school?"

"I was suspended the other day."

"The hell you say! What for?"

"A fight. I cut Clay Sanger's ear."

"Uh-huh. Was it over the girl?"

"Yeah."

Kevin was uncomfortable under Birdsong's gaze and his questions. The weariness had left his voice. The questions were cold, flat, as if Birdsong were a lawyer and Kevin his witness.

"You got a job?"

"No."

"You going back to school?"

"Sure."

"Good boy! You ought to get that education. You know what? Jasper's studying like crazy. He never studied at home the way he is down there."

"That's great!"

"I'm proud of him. Say, what's your girl's name? She's a Hawthorne, isn't she?"

"Yeah. Rosa Hawthorne. Carmelita's daughter."

"Oh. Gregorio's granddaughter?"

"Yes."

"How *is* old Gregorio?"

"He stays on his side of Star Mountain. I haven't seen him since I went to the ranch."

"I wish the old buzzard would write me. I don't know what the hell's going on around there anymore. Jimmy George never wrote, either. I'd call him, but he was so scared of the damn phone he wouldn't say anything. Old Jimmy George. He was a good one."

"The best. I used to work with him some."

"That's right, you did!"

"In the summers."

"Yeah, I remember." He looked out the window at the desert darkness. "Well, with him gone and Emmy gone, that just leaves old Gregorio and a couple of wetbacks out there. I ought to be out there myself, but Vera thinks we should stay with Jasper. I guess she's right."

Kevin said nothing. He stared straight down the highway, dimming his lights for a semi gunning for El Paso. Birdsong fell silent, too, and Kevin thought he might have gone to sleep. He turned and looked, and Birdsong was staring down the highway, too. He took Kevin's glance as a cue. "How would you like to work for me?" he asked.

Kevin shrugged. "I've worked for you before."

"You speak Spanish?"

215

"Some."

"Why don't you and your girl move into Jimmy George's house? It's not too far to drive to school. You could use Jasper's car. I'll give you a hundred dollars a month and charge accounts at the grocery store and gas station. And the house, of course."

"For doing what?"

"Nothing much, this winter. Just keep the place from falling apart. Keep the cows from starving. Keep them off the highway. There'll be more work in the spring. And more money. I just need somebody with a few brains. Somebody that'll take a little responsibility."

"I'd like to think about it."

"You got a better offer?"

"No. I'd just like to talk to my wife about it."

"Oh. Sure. But remember, you're going to have another mouth to feed pretty soon."

"I remember."

"It's a good offer."

"It sounds good."

"Will you take it?"

"I want to talk to Rosa first."

"Okay. But let me know before I go back to Gonzales. I've got to find somebody."

"I will."

"That's all I ask. You mind if I take a little nap? I'm really whipped."

"No. Go right ahead."

"You can play the radio if you get sleepy. It's got a good tone. It'll pick up just about any station."

"Okay, if I get sleepy. I'm not sleepy now, though."

"Well, goodnight."

"Goodnight, sir."

Birdsong tilted his hat over his eyes and scooted forward

until his head was resting on the back of the seat. "Thank you for driving all this way," he said.

"De nada," Kevin replied.

Four

Rosa was surprised at how clean Jimmy George had left the place. She changed the sheets on the iron bed and washed the dishes he had left on the kitchen table. She removed his few clothes from the drawers of the bureau and the old wardrobe in the corner and folded them into a box for the next Holy Name Society rummage sale. He had no family. He left no will. Carl Birdsong had told Kevin to give away anything he didn't want to keep. The only things of value she had found among his possessions were an almost new black hat on the shelf in the wardrobe and a pair of good boots under the bed. She laid the hat on top of the clothing in the box. The boots fit Kevin, and he was keeping them. Birdsong had also given him Jimmy George's spurs, saddle, blanket, bridle, and Winchester carbine.

The house was a flat-roofed, unstuccoed adobe hut, so old that its corners curved inward from decades of the wind's erosion. Rosa had been inside a dozen like it in Little Juarez, all dirt-floored and filthy. But Jimmy George's walls were stuccoed and whitewashed, with no muddy streaks bespeaking leaks in the roof. The gray cobblestone floor glowed. The cast-iron wood stove at the end of the room and the gunmetal-blue stovepipe that curved into the wall were almost new. The iron bed and the little table beside it, the rocker by the stove and the little table beside it, the huge carved wardrobe, and the big bureau with the mirror were old but strong. Jimmy George had even hung curtains over the windows, burlap feed sacks, folded over curtain rods and pinned with horseshoe nails. The kitchen was long and narrow, with old, but clean, gas range and refrigerator flanking an old-fashioned sink with a burlap curtain around the bottom. A small, oilclothed table and one chair stood at one end, under a window. And through the door that had once been the hut's back door was a small bathroom, built of gray cinder-block, with a shower. It was so new that the cinder-block had not yet been painted. Even the woodpile, which Rosa could see through the window over the sink, was near the house and abundant with hard, long-burning oak.

When she had put away their clothes and plugged in her small lamp beside the bed, and laid her ragged old dog on the pillows, their move was complete, except for Kevin's books. Mary Beth had left her house while they moved them. Rosa and Kevin packed them hastily and carried them to the Circle-B pickup. Now his large bookcase stood against the wall between the front door and the window, but the books still lay in their boxes on the cobblestones. Kevin had told Rosa not to touch them. They had to be arranged on the shelves in a certain way that she didn't know.

Rosa enjoyed the roar of the fire in the stove and the pattern the sunlight and the curtains made across the floor. With a few more chairs, she would be comfortable here.

The loud knock startled her. She ran to open the door. Gregorio grinned and spread his arms wide. "I thought this ranch was cursed, but now an angel has come!" he exclaimed, folding her into his bear hug.

"Good morning, Grandpapa." She kissed his cheek.

"May I come in?"

"Of course. You need no invitation, silly."

Gregorio stepped inside, removed his hat and tossed it

218

on the bed. He unbuttoned his sheepskin jacket and warmed his backside at the stove and looked around him. "Yes, I can tell that a woman lives here."

"Oh, Grandpapa! It's just as Jimmy George left it."

He grinned. "Yes, but *you* are here." He swept his arm over the room. "How do you like it?"

"It's lovely. I feel at home here."

"You should. Your great-grandfather built it."

"Really?"

"Yes. It's the oldest house on the ranch. I was born in this room. The bed was in the same place. I remember it."

"Oh, Grandpapa!"

They laughed.

"Where is your man?"

"At the corral, I think."

"How is he?"

"He's fine."

"I mean, is he a *good* man?"

"Yes, he *is* a good man."

"He's a *gringo.*"

Rosa grinned impishly. "Your father was a *gringo,* too, no?"

"But it was different then."

"Well, it's different now, too."

Gregorio chuckled, shaking his head. "Are you . . ." He cradled his arms and rocked them.

"Yes. I'm pregnant."

"It surprises me that he married you. To *gringos,* a pregnant Mexican is nothing."

"I told you. He's a *good* man."

"Good. I'm glad. Is he going to be the new *jefe?*"

"I don't know. Maybe that's what Mr. Birdsong has in mind."

"Your man's young. He has a lot to learn."

219

"Yes, he does. Will you teach him?"

Gregorio gazed at the scuffed toes of his boots. "Yes, I'll teach him."

"Thank you, Grandpapa."

"Will you go to school?"

"Yes, Grandpapa."

"The baby . . ."

"The baby won't come before school is out. This is my last year, you know. I'm graduating."

"And your man?"

"He's graduating, too. He and I and Emmy were in the same class, Grandpapa."

"Ah, yes. He's a good football player, isn't he?"

"Yes, he is."

"I'll help him then." Gregorio grinned and threw up his hands. "It's *good* to have a woman on this ranch again."

Rosa giggled. "Mrs. Birdsong has been here a long time."

Gregorio snorted. "She's a dried up old cow!"

They laughed.

"It'll be good to have a strong young man here, too," he said. "I'm very old, you know."

"You're not so old. Find a wife and make more sons."

Gregorio smiled sadly. "Oh, no. Oh, no. I'm through with that. I must go now and find your man." He buttoned his coat and picked up his hat. He didn't put it on until he was outside the door.

"You're welcome here," Rosa said. "Come again at night and sit with us. You'll be welcome."

Gregorio squinted at her and nodded. "It's a long way to the other side of the mountain at night, but I'll do it. I must find your man now."

Rosa closed the door and stood with her back to the fire, as Gregorio had done, and looked at the bed. She wondered if it had really been in that spot. She smiled. She felt very much at home.

MARCH, 1953

One

Kevin eased the Cadillac up to the stone front steps. He took the wheelchair out of the trunk and unfolded it and helped Jasper get settled into it. He and Carl Birdsong carried it up the steep steps and set it on the long, shady porch, where a glass wind chime tinkled. Jasper peered thoughtfully at the chime, then down the brown lane toward Leaping Panther Mountain looming over the silver courthouse dome and the little stores. Kevin and Carl and Vera Birdsong watched him, Kevin and Birdsong smiling, Vera frowning, twisting a lace handkerchief around her fingers.

Jasper looked up at Kevin. "Thank you, buddy."

"It's nothing. I'm one of the hired hands now."

Jasper frowned.

"I'd better get the luggage in." Kevin bounded down the steps and lifted three large suitcases out of the trunk. "Is this all?"

"We shipped the rest," Birdsong said. "Just put it in the hall."

Kevin set the suitcases under the gun rack in the hall and returned to the porch.

"You want me to move the car, Mr. Birdsong?"

"No. Just close the trunk and leave it."

Kevin extended his hand to Jasper. "I'd better get back to the ranch. It's good to have you back."

Jasper shook his hand solemnly, but said nothing until Kevin started down the steps again.

"Kevin?"

"Yeah?"

"Come see me tonight."

"Okay. I'll bring Rosa."

"Not tonight, okay? I'd like a visit with you alone."

"Yeah, we do have a lot of catching up to do, don't we?"
Jasper nodded.

Kevin was about to ring the doorbell when Jasper called his name out of the darkness. He was sitting under the wind chime.

"Hey, man, you been sitting there all day?"

"No. I figured we could talk better out here. I wanted to get away from the folks. They're driving me nuts."

Kevin found a lawn chair against the wall and dragged it up beside Jasper's wheelchair. Jasper pointed to a carton perched on the porch rail. "The churchkey's on top."

The beer was no longer cold. It foamed over Kevin's hand when he punctured the tops of the cans. He handed one to Jasper and sucked the foam off the top of his own.

"I haven't had a beer since I left town," Jasper said.

"That's a long time, buddy."

"Yeah." He paused, then pointed into the darkness. "I was remembering that time Emmy swam with us down there. You remember that?"

"Sure."

"When was that?"

"Last summer."

"Jesus. A lot of water has passed under the bridge since then. Or a lot has passed into the tank, I guess."

"It's empty. Somebody drained it after . . ."

"Is that where they think I got it?"

"I don't know. We were scared. We did a lot of things."

Jasper sucked at his beer. Kevin was counting on his fingers the months that had passed since that swim. Only

226

seven. Now his oldest friend seemed a stranger. He didn't know what to say to him. Should he ask about his months in the hospitals? About his disease and his treatment? He didn't want to know about them. He didn't know whether Jasper wanted to talk about them. Should he tell Jasper about Rosa? About the Old Fort and the cottonwoods? About Carmelita? About Clay Sanger? About Alicia? About Willie Joe Callahan? Would Jasper want to hear about Juanito Rodriguez and Emmy and the funerals?

Jasper chuckled hoarsely. "I know what you're thinking. Don't feel sorry for me. This polio may be the best thing that ever happened to me."

"Why?" Kevin asked softly.

Jasper waved his arm over the darkened landscape. "I hate this. I hate this town. I hate the ranch. I hate cows. I hate looking at the sky and wishing for rain. Now I don't have to do any of it. Now Daddy can't ship me off to A&M for a year and then drag me back. I'll never have to pull another cow out of a mudhole or scoop the maggots out of her eyes. I've got *freedom* now. The polio gave it to me."

"Someday you'll own the place. You'll just tell *me* to do those things."

"You're not *staying*, are you?"

"For a while. I like it."

"You'll hate it later."

"I like it now."

"You like working for a hundred a month?"

"Your dad says I'll get more later."

Jasper snorted. "Not much more. He's got you in mind for the new Jimmy George. I can see us fifty years from now, me sitting here in Levis and boots with braces, and you standing there with your hat in your hand, telling me your wife's sick, asking to borrow fifty bucks. That's not for me, buddy. I'm getting out."

"Getting out?"

"Going to Princeton, I hope. Maybe the University of Texas. I'm going to get me a degree in business administration and a job in an air-conditioned office with elevators. Fuck the droughts. Bye-bye, Fort Appleby. If my old man doesn't like it, I can just point to my legs and say, 'What you going to do about it, honey?' I got freedom." He lifted the can and finished the beer. "Open me another one. Why don't you come with me?"

"I'm a family man now, and not rich."

They sat quietly, studying the wedge-shaped holes in their beer cans, feeling the alcohol course through their arteries, listening to the chime tinkle in the breeze. Jasper sighed and hurled his half-full can over the railing.

"Well, shit," he said. "What else is there to say?"

Two

Kevin and Rosa went to Eisenbarger's office together. They sat down on the two chairs that Eisenbarger had placed side-by-side in front of his desk. They glanced at each other when Eisenbarger walked around them and closed the door.

"Well, thanks for coming," Eisenbarger said.

"You sent for us," Kevin said.

Eisenbarger maneuvered his swivel chair up to his desk and clasped his hands in front of his face, as if praying. He glanced at Kevin, then at Rosa. "How are you, Rosa?"

"I'm fine, Mr. Jay." She smiled at him.

"That's good. That's fine." His eyes left hers and wandered upward to a nail hammered into the facing above the door, where he hung a sprig of mistletoe at Christmastime.

"Well, kids, I'm afraid I have bad news for you. The school board wants Rosa to leave school."

Kevin sneered. "I don't need to ask why, but I will."

"She's pregnant. She's showing now. Everybody knows it."

"And?"

"And the board says she's setting a bad moral example for the other girls."

"Rosa's *married!*"

Rosa squeezed Kevin's arm. He looked at her. She frowned and shook her head.

"I told them that every one of them had children in wedlock, and I didn't consider them immoral for it, even though I knew their children. I'm afraid they didn't catch my humor. Anyway, they established a policy that pregnant students have to leave school, married or not."

"And what about the *fathers* of all those babies?" Kevin asked.

"The fathers may remain, married or not, provided they keep their hands off of the other girls."

"I won't stay. If Rosa goes, I do, too."

Eisenbarger nodded. "I thought you might say that. The board agreed to let you finish your courses at home. We'll mail your diplomas to you."

"I won't do that, either," Kevin said. "To hell with all of it."

Eisenbarger glared. "You *will* do it, ass! I put my job on the line for you. I said I would resign if they barred you from getting your diploma. And you're going to get it, by God, if I have to drive out to that ranch every night and stand over you with a gun until you get those assignments done!" He shifted his glare to Rosa. "That goes for you, too, young lady!"

Rosa smiled. "I'll hold the gun when you get tired."

Eisenbarger relaxed and smiled at her. "Fine," he said. "Go clean out your lockers. You may pick up your assignments at my house whenever you come to town, and leave your homework there. Now get out of here."

Kevin, still glowering, remained seated.

"Get out of here, stupid," Eisenbarger said. "Do whatever the lady says."

MAY, 1953

One

"You going to start this summer?"

"No. Graduation's not till the end of June. Summer school will start before that. I'll wait till September, then to Austin."

"I'll bet you're already packing."

"No, but I'm making lists."

The old Ford's door was open. Jasper sat on the end of the seat, his elbow on the steering wheel. Kevin hunkered on the ground by the door, his straw hat pushed back. He struck a match on the seat of his Levis and lit a cigarette.

"Where'd you learn that?" Jasper asked.

"Gregorio taught me."

Rosa appeared at the screen door. "Want some coffee?"

"Yeah. Bring it out here, hon."

Jasper snickered. "Jesus! Listen to the old married man!"

Kevin grinned self-consciously. "I *am* an old married man. I like it, too."

"Really?"

Rosa carried two large mugs to the car. "It's black," she said to Jasper. "Do you need anything?"

"No." Jasper touched her belly. "Is it ripe yet?"

"No, but it's kicking."

"I don't believe you're really pregnant."

Rosa clapped her hand over his mouth. "Don't tell the idiot!"

Jasper watched her walk back to the house. "You *are* happy, aren't you?"

"Yes."

"I never would have figured it."

"Neither would I."

"When the old man kicks off, I'll make you a partner."

Kevin laughed. "Bullshit!"

"I'm serious. I don't want the damn thing."

"Give me *all* of it, then."

Jasper smiled. "I don't want to be poor, either. No, you wait. Someday this place will be half yours."

"Aw, bullshit, Jasper!"

"I can't let you be a hundred-a-month cowboy all your life! You'll be doing me a favor, anyway."

"Aw, shit, Jasper."

"You don't believe me, huh?"

"Oh, you *mean* it, all right. But things happen. You'll change your mind."

"You want it in writing?"

Kevin squinted up at Jasper. The brown eyes in the thin face challenged him. "Naw," he said.

"Well, will you shake with me on it?" Jasper extended his hand.

Kevin rose and stepped stiffly to the car, and they shook on it.

JULY, 1953

One

A hand shook him roughly. His mind climbed slowly, reluctantly out of its deep sleep. He frowned and opened his eyes, blinking in the glare of the lamp. Silhouetted against the glare was the face of Carmelita. "Wake up, Kevin. Look at your son."

He jumped up and looked around him, confused. At the door a nurse stood, her mask hanging around her neck. Beside her was a little glass case on legs with wheels. The baby wasn't moving. It was smaller than he had expected, and very red. "Is it all right?"

"Oh, yes, he's fine," the nurse said. "He has all his fingers and toes."

"Fingers and toes?"

"That's what dads always ask about. You look awfully young. I didn't believe you were the father until your maid told me."

"She's my mother-in-law."

The nurse blushed. "Sorry. He weighs eight pounds two ounces and is twenty-one inches long. That's another thing dads ask."

"Is that big, or little, or what?"

"It's a nice, healthy size. He's a nice baby, Mr. Adams."

Kevin peered through the glass again. He wondered how women could tell about such things. He glanced at the nurse, who was watching him with curiosity in her eyes, a slight smile on her lips. Carmelita beamed with the superiority that women always feel when they watch men with babies.

"I have to take him to the nursery, Mr. Adams. You can see him again later."

"How's my wife?"

"She's fine. She came through it in good shape."

"May I see her?"

"In a little while. We put her out. She won't make much sense for a while."

The nurse wheeled the case away. Carmelita hugged him. "Congratulations, Papa. Papa needs some coffee. Then he can go see Rosa." She took his hand and led him to the small, dimly lit cafeteria. Nobody was in the room. A large urn sat on a table to the side. Carmelita filled two cups and carried them to a table. "Well, how do you feel?"

Kevin rubbed his temples. "Why did you let me go to sleep?"

"You've been here a long time."

"What time is it?"

"Five-thirty in the morning."

"Damn! I was hoping he would come on the Fourth of July."

"You should have told him. Maybe he would have hurried. Be thankful that he's a beautiful boy."

"Is he really?"

"Yes. Beautiful. Do you have a name for him?"

"Jasper Hawthorne Adams."

"A beautiful name, too." When they finished their coffee, she guided him to the door of the recovery room. "Your mother called," she said. "Before the baby came. She wants you to call her."

"You call her."

"What should I tell her?"

"Anything."

Carmelita remained outside while Kevin went in. Rosa's

white hospital gown was wrinkled and disheveled. A nurse sat beside her. Rosa's face glistened with sweat. Her head tossed and rolled.

"Is she all right?"

"Yes," the nurse said. "She just hasn't come around yet."

Kevin bent close to her. "Rosa?"

"Get your filthy hands off!"

"That's the sweetest thing she's said all night," the nurse said. "She was a real tiger."

Kevin picked up Rosa's hand and kissed it. "Tell her I'll come back later."

"Is she awake?" Carmelita asked.

"No."

"Go home and get some sleep. Take a bath and shave and dress up. Give Rosa a chance to get beautiful for you."

"Are you staying here?"

"Of course. What's a grandmother for?"

Kevin walked into the parking lot. Dawn was lighting the horizon. The still air was so cool that he shivered. His head still felt stuffy and lifeless. As he steered the pickup through the empty streets of Sharon, he rolled down the window. The cool air refreshed him. He floorboarded the pickup across the flat toward the mountains.

Gregorio was walking toward the corral. When he heard the clank of the tailgate chains, he stopped and waited. The pickup sped around the curve and skidded to a stop. Kevin sprang from the cab and embraced him.

"Gregorio! You're a great-grandfather today!"

"Praise God!"

"It's a boy!"

"Praise God!"

239

They broke their embrace and gazed upon one another, pride burning in their eyes. Then Kevin said, "I need to ride. Will you come with me?"

They saddled Jimmy George's big roan and Emiliano's pinto. Kevin mounted and whipped the roan around the headquarters house toward the trail that wound up the hill with the grove of oaks on its crest. Gregorio pulled abreast on the little pinto. The horses, unaccustomed to working so hard so early, grunted up the steep slope. Their riders slowed them to a walk as they passed the graves of Rafael and Dietrich and Juanito, and reined in beyond the trees, at the edge of the precipice. The horses snorted. The first rays of the sun were bursting over the long crest of Leaping Panther Mountain. Shadows moved in Victorio Canyon and among the lower hills.